I0717989

The Derbyshire Set ~ Book 6

Regency Historical Romance

The Marquess Scandalous Mistress

Arietta Richmond

Dreamstone Publishing © 2016

www.dreamstonepublishing.com

Books by Arietta Richmond

His Majesty's Hounds

Claiming the Heart of a Duke

Intriguing the Viscount

Giving a Heart of Lace (a prequel to Winning the Merchant Earl)

Being Lady Harriet's Hero

Enchanting the Duke (coming soon)

Redeeming the Marquess (coming soon)

Healing Lord Barton (coming soon)

Winning the Merchant Earl (coming soon)

Loving the Bitter Baron (coming soon)

Rescuing the Countess (coming soon)

Attracting the Spymaster (coming soon)

The Derbyshire Set

A Gift of Love (Prequel short story)

A Devil's Bargain (Prequel short story - coming soon)

The Earl's Unexpected Bride

The Captain's Compromised Heiress

The Viscount's Unsuitable Affair

The Count's Impetuous Seduction

The Rake's Unlikely Redemption

The Marquess' Scandalous Mistress

A Remembered Face (Bonus short story – coming soon)

The Marchioness' Second Chance (coming soon)

A Viscount's Reluctant Passion (coming soon)

Lady Theodora's Christmas Wish

The Duke's Improper Love (coming soon)

Other Books

The Scottish Governess (coming soon)

The Earl's Reluctant Fiancée (coming soon)

The Crew of the Seadragon's Soul Series, (coming soon - a set of 10 linked novels)

ARIETTA RICHMOND

Dedication

For everyone who had the grace to be patient while this book, and the ones before and after it, were coming into existence, who provided cups of tea, and food, when the writing would not let me go, and endured countless times being asked for opinions.

For the readers coming to know these characters well, and who inspire me to continue, by buying my books!

For my growing team of beta readers and advance reviewers – it's thanks to you that others can enjoy these books in the best presentation possible!

And for all the writers of Regency Historical Romance, whose books I read, who inspired me to write in this fascinating period.

Chapter One

"Well" said Lady Olivia Asterwood, Marchioness Hemsbridge, her voice becoming somewhat shrill, a reflection of the intense frustration that she was repressing, "- you're going to have to find a wife sometime, Sterling my boy, you're nearly thirty now, after all, and tonight should present as good an opportunity as any."

"Yes mother, indeed it shall" replied her son, Sterling Asterwood, Marquess Hemsbridge, in a voice which was flat and lacking any conviction.

This was a speech that he had heard so often he could probably have quoted it verbatim if requested. Since he'd been barely out of swaddling clothes and away from his nanny's bosom his mother had been pressing him towards the skirt-hems of young ladies, whispering 'matrimony' from afar, without the barest hint of subtlety.

It was her obsession, her *raison d'etre,* her first vague notion in the morning sunlight and her final quivering half-thought before sleep. She was obsessed with maintaining their bloodline, and with the genealogy of the aristocracy in general.

"I simply can't understand it Sterling" she rambled on, undeterred by his outward lack of interest. "We never had any of these difficulties with Tobias, or Gloriana for that matter.

Both your siblings managed to fall into suitable matches in no time at all, yet that achievement seems to have defeated you. And you being the eldest everyone expected you to do your duty first. Most peculiar, I'm afraid to say, it's the talk of the county balls."

"I don't give a jot what they say at your blasted balls mother!" Sterling snapped back. "This is my own life and, at present, I am quite satisfied with the liberties of bachelorhood." It was only half a lie.

Of course the Marquess of Hemsbridge wanted a Marchioness, eventually. Of course he woke up in the mornings wishing the cold pillow beside him was supporting the warmth of a pretty young head.

Of course he pursued women, girls, ladies, pretty, plain - all manner of women, at the balls he managed to get to without his mildly outrageous mother in tow, and he certainly achieved some pleasant results from his pursuit.

Just not the sort of results that he wished to share with his mother, nor the sort that ever seemed to lead to the ringing sound of wedding bells.

"It's not that you aren't handsome, my boy," said the Marchioness, pinching his cheek in what she mistakenly believed to be an affectionate gesture (it had ceased to be so when he was about six…), "handsome and charming to boot, with feet that can dance and a tongue that can talk. Too picky is what you are, picky as a Reverend with an upset stomach, as my nanny used to say. Lord knows what she meant, but you shouldn't take that attitude about me, or Somerset society for that matter. If you want to make your way out of the doldrums of bachelorhood and into the sweet harbour of marriage, you shall have to depend on both."

"Yes mother, as you wish." Hemsbridge ran his fingers through his lush copper brown hair, only to find a knot which he could not seem to push through. The effort hurt, but his mother did not notice his grimace of pain.

"Why, I must say…" she blurted, after sipping the last of her afternoon tea. She was rather enjoying herself, sitting in the drawing room, supping at sweet, milky tea and lecturing her son. "… had I been as picky as you are, Sterling, when I was in my twenties, I'd never have married your father, oh good god no! He was a right clodhopper, with two left feet and no conversation whatsoever. But still, he was handsome enough, had a fortune that was at least commensurate with my dynastic expectations, and that was that. I did what was to be done, for my family name, and for my unborn infants. And now here you are."

"Your generosity does you credit, my lady." Hemsbridge muttered sarcastically. At times like this, a small part of him wished she'd never bothered.

"Duty my boy, duty, that's the most important thing. It matters more than anything. More than any pretty face, or well-cut dress, or a successful afternoon's cavorting at the Derby. Duty to one's family, to one's future, to one's ancestors, to what went before and what is still to come. Without a firm commitment to duty, you shall die not only lonely, but also without issue, and more than just you shall be dead, Sterling Asterwood, your family will die too. The great coat of arms emblazoned on your doorway, the rich blue blood that flows in your veins, the name that you were born too, all will cease to be. Never forget it, it is all infinitely more important than any paltry rot you read in books about love and romance. Those things are all well and good when you're young and have no commitments, but in time, one must realise what is important, and keep the good ship Hemsbridge afloat."

"Most insightful of you mother - Aristotle, I feel, could not have put it better. But now, if you'll excuse me, I have pheasants to be shooting." He rose to his feet rapidly, but was quickly returned to the embrace of the plump armchair he'd been occupying by his mother's stick. She flicked it up at him with an agility that defied the concept that she needed to use it, which indeed she did not — it was an affectation on her part - and used it to prod him back to a seated position.

"Oh no, you will not be shooting pheasant this afternoon, my good Marquess Hemsbridge!" she declared, emboldened by his look of confusion. "There is another sort of bird entirely you shall be hunting tonight, at the Duke of Whitehaven's ball. You shall eschew the cheap thrills of the chase for the hunting of another breed of prey entirely: a suitable wife!"

Hemsbridge rolled his eyes, considered protesting or running away, declined to bother with either, and resigned himself to another night of stilted conservation amongst Somerset society, in the presence of his dearly beloved mother.

"Ooh, that's Lady Arianna Betstaff!" exclaimed the Marchioness Hemsbridge, between mouthfuls of ratafia.

"Wonderful match, don't you think, such an eligible young lady. Her roots go deep, all the way back to William the Conqueror I hear. She's the talk of the West Country."

"Is she indeed?" Hemsbridge mumbled. He glanced over at the young lady but was not deeply impressed. She had a face that was too round, like a dinner plate someone had decorated with a muddy blonde wig. Her demeanour and mannerisms gave her the look of a girl who spends a bit too much time laughing along with men's jokes and presuming friendship, a trait that he had never found attractive.

"That girl behind her is at least as eligible too!" his mother continued, undeterred.

"The wealthiest heiress in the county, and one of the wealthiest in the kingdom, I'll wager. Lady Amelia Castleford, wonderful girl, I hear her father recently inherited the Ockington estate. Their coffers must be overflowing." The Marchioness seemed to lick her lips at the thought of all the Castleford gold, but all Hemsbridge could see was the wart on the girl's rather too long nose. *Eligible for a more cash-strapped and desperate bachelor than I,* he thought, *but not for me.*

"Mercy me, I fear I shall faint at the sight of all these wonderful young ladies!" said the Marchioness, swaying slightly and trying to keep from broadcasting her insights to the entire room. "Lady Lavinia Witherwood, our host's daughter. Why, isn't she a picture? I shall have to introduce you." Hemsbridge almost let out a most impolite sound as his mother grabbed hold of his arm, pinching it in the process, and led him, rather haughtily, towards Lady Lavinia, where she stood beside her father. As he eyed her, he felt a limited optimism rising within him. The girl was very small for her age it was true, but in the pearly white dress she was wearing, setting off her golden hair, she was rather pretty, in a frail sort of way.

"Your Grace," Hemsbridge's mother said, in the firmer voice she used to communicate with people beyond her immediate family. "May I present my son, the Marquess of Hemsbridge."

"My Lord." Whitehaven said, bowing. He was a tall man with a stern profile, like a general or an especially clever city lawyer. His hair was thinning on top to reveal a rather unsightly red patch, but he had an otherwise distinguished appearance. Hemsbridge duly returned the greeting.

"It is a pleasure to have such esteemed guests in attendance. This is, I fear, only a modest gathering of country society, but my hope is that it shall suffice."

"Oh, certainly my lord, I would not fear, you have assembled such a group of notables as East Somerset has never before witnessed!"

"My Lady is too kind, of course, but immodest as I am, I shall accept your compliment." Hemsbridge, rapidly losing interest in this exchange of formality, was discreetly studying young Lavinia. She returned his glance, and seemed to blush rather girlishly before turning away.

"But where are my manners? May I present my daughter, Lady Lavinia Witherwood." Lady Lavinia turned and curtsied, with a sweet smile that revealed her dimples. "The Marquess of Hemsbridge, and his mother, the Marchioness."

"Charmed" said Hemsbridge casually, bending to kiss Lavinia's hand. She was so frail and retiring that he felt that, if a servant were to open a window, she might be carried away in the ensuing gust of wind.

"My pleasure, Lord Hemsbridge" she just about managed to say. Hemsbridge had to lean forward sharply to make out her words. Her voice was frail and trembling, as if she were lowering herself into a pool of iced water every time she spoke. He noticed her father glance at him expectantly, aiming for the sort of comradely look men often exchange in the presence of attractive ladies. Simultaneously, his mother was nodding at him, far less subtly, to indicate approval. He knew at once that he had no choice but to ask the girl to dance, though he felt little enthusiasm at the prospect.

"Lady Lavinia, it seems the logical choice at this point; would you do me the honour of granting me a dance? That is, of course, if you have any openings on your dance card?" Present company assumed that he was a little stiff in his comment about choice. If only they knew his real opinion, he thought to himself.

"Oh! Oh yes sir, it would be a great pleasure. As it happens, I do have this next dance free."

"Wonderful, then let us proceed." He held out his hand, received another encouraging nod from his mother and his host, and with a wince he just about managed to suppress, took Lady Lavinia's clammy little hand in his and placed it on his arm.

*

As Hemsbridge had very much anticipated, Lavinia Witherwood was not much of a dancer. Her efforts were confounded by a combination of timidity and a waifish, unphysicality that did not lend itself well to this sort of rhythmic exercise. Hemsbridge fancied, from her demeanour, that she was the sort of girl who picked at her food interminably, who preferred green vegetables to a good slab of red meat, who did not care for loud music or strong drink and who mounted a horse rarely and with great trepidation.

Had he had the time to enquire, of one of her intimate associates, on any or all of these questions, he would have discovered that he was correct on all counts and more. She was not, in any sense, a spirited girl.

"Tell me, my Lady" Hemsbridge asked, feigning an interest in his dance partner. "What subjects compel your interest? What occupies the mind of the Duke of Whitehaven's pretty young daughter?" She blushed uncontrollably at this compliment, tame as it was.

"Why sir, little that would be of much interest to an important gentleman such as yourself. I have a great fondness for needlework, and devote much of my time to its practice. It is but a simple pastime, but it occupies the body and mind as required."

"Scintillating" Hemsbridge managed to squeeze out the word, trying not to roll his eyes. This was at least his third attempt to steer their conversation out of the gentle, shallow waters of chit-chat and into the great blue sea of excitement he was seeking, but Lavinia would not oblige.

"I also take bracing walks on the seafront when I can. I find that to be a most invigorating diversion."

"Wonderful. Sea air does one good I suppose?"

"Oh yes sir! It is superb for the constitution!" It took all of Hemsbridge's strength of will to suppress a yawn at this tedious insight. This girl might one day make a fine match for a quiet, timid sort of a chap, he thought, perhaps a vicar, or the underachieving fifth son of some run-of-the-mill minor household. She was not, however, the sort of woman who could interest him.

Just as these thoughts were running through his mind, he saw a woman of a very different type, moving boldly across the room.

This was more the sort of woman in whom he could feel an interest! She was tall, with a slender physique, the shape of which could be determined, even in her evening gown. Her slim waist, flaring to well-shaped hips immediately struck him. Her hair, intricately coiffed, sat high upon her head and shimmered golden in the evening's candlelight. She had a certain energy about her, as if the world held little in it that could possibly cause her fear or distress. Gentlemen's heads turned all at once, like willows swaying in unison in the wind, glancing at her, momentarily ignoring the other women in the room. She ghosted through the crush like a wisp, then headed out onto the terrace and was gone. Hemsbridge turned back to his tedious dance partner, who now seemed all the less appealing for being compared to the unknown woman who had just passed through his view.

"You will excuse me, my lady" he said with a slight bow, uncoupling his hands from Lavinia's trembling fingers, as the dance mercifully came to an end. "But I have a pressing need to converse with an associate. A most mundane matter, but necessary, I'm afraid, you will excuse me." The girl whimpered something like "but of course my lord", but Hemsbridge did not tarry long enough to hear it. He moved suddenly with a singular force, slipping across the crowded room, on the trail of that woman who had just caught his eye, interested in no-one and nothing else.

*

Hemsbridge was disappointed to see that the mysterious woman was not, as her earlier course would have suggested, out on the terrace, but was, instead, nowhere to be seen.

He scanned his surrounds, trying as hard as he could not to appear odd in front of the other guests, who were enjoying the air on the terrace.

He quickly realised that she was definitely not there, was, in fact, not anywhere, that he could see.

A middle-aged fellow, with the ruddy look of a man who's indulged in a little too much port, who was outside talking to a girl half his age, turned to him with a look of concern.

"Is everything quite alright, my Lord? You appear to have lost something?"

"I'm fine, thank you. I thought that I had seen someone I know come out here, but it appears I was mistaken." Hemsbridge was muttering, without even turning to make eye contact. "I am now simply taking in some of this fine evening air."

"Got a little stuffy in the ballroom, eh?" the man replied, jokingly, in a tone Hemsbridge did not much care for. "Well I can't say I blame you, there are some handsome ladies in attendance tonight, make no mistake. Why I just saw one of them, slipping through here, popping off with some gentleman friend of hers, out into the gardens. I think I may have some idea of what they had in mind, though it would be neither proper, nor gentlemanly, of me to say so, what?!"

The fellow guffawed idiotically, turning Hemsbridge yet further against him. The girl he was with tittered in response to this salacious speculation, but Hemsbridge turned to them. Here was a source of information.

"Did you see where they went?" he asked as calmly as he could, trying to sound as if it was of little import to him.

"Gosh old chap, I don't see it's any of your business is it? Unless she's a lover of yours and you're being made a cuckold, in which case I'm afraid the game is already up!" He punctuated his speak with another raucous laugh, as if this was quite the most amusing idea he had had all evening. "They headed over to those trees yonder, if you must know."

"The trees? And who was the man she was with? What did he look like?" Sterling felt an irrational surge of jealousy, which was very strange and completely inappropriate – after all, he had only seen the woman once, across a crowded room, and she did not even know that he existed.

"Good grief, I don't know, and I don't quite understand why you care, my good man. But let me think a moment, seeing as you ask. Hmmm…. yes,… he was sort of tall, dark hair, wearing a red cravat I seem to recall, most unusual."

At this, Hemsbridge's eyes grew wide, and he took a sharp intake of breath. The man he was talking to stepped back, looking a little alarmed at his intensity.

"Was his nose crooked? Positioned oddly to the side like he'd been kicked by a half wild stallion?"

"I only saw him for a second old chap! I wasn't looking out for these sorts of details… though come to mention it, I do believe his nose was rather funny, yes. 'Distinguishing features' I suppose a magistrate might say. This is rather fun, actually, isn't it, working all this out?"

But Hemsbridge did not reply.

He was staring intently into the distance, over towards the trees, where, just this moment, he now knew that the only woman at this ball who could interest him at all was being ravished by a rake, a scoundrel, a bounder, a fellow he had known for many years and with whom he had shared many nights of companionship, and many of sin.

"Aldercott" he muttered at last. "Braydon bloody Aldercott, the bastard."

"I say, do you know this fellow?"

"Of course I know him. I know him rather too well for my liking, or anyone else's for that matter. The swine." Sterling knew that the intensity of his reaction was not rational, that, if he considered it, any woman who would voluntarily go off into the bushes with Aldercott was most likely not very well behaved at all – certainly not a woman whose 'honour' needed defending!

"I say old boy, are you alright?" the man said, abandoning his female companion for a moment, quite distracted by Hemsbridge's intensity.

"You look like you could do with a glass of something stiffer than punch! How about a scotch? I'll have my man fetch you one at once, you look like you've seen a ghost!"

"I haven't. It's quite alright, I'm sure the rascal will skulk back in to explain himself in due course. Farewell." Leaving his companions even more confused than when he had first burst onto the terrace, Hemsbridge returned to the ball.

*

"Do you read scripture at all, Lord Hemsbridge?" said Lady Thrapston, in a shrill tone that made no apologies. The young woman was dowdy and stout, and had planted her arm firmly behind Hemsbridge's back.

"Alas, I find I seldom have the time these days" he replied, giving what he hoped would prove a diplomatic answer.

"No time for the word of God?! Good Lord, what in Heaven or Earth can be the matter with you? I consider any day that does not begin and end on my knees before the Heavenly Father to be not only wasted, but sinful!"

"An admirable conviction, my Lady."

"Well, I should hope so! Where would we be without the redeeming light of Christ?"

"Where indeed?" Hemsbridge wanted nothing more than to get away, and fast. This one was far worse than Lavinia Witherwood! The former might have been dull, but at least she wasn't a religious zealot.

"Have you a favourite passage in the Book of Matthew, Lord Hemsbridge?" Lady Thrapston asked, staring at him with what could only be described as fanatical aggression.

"Matthew?" he said, casting about in the back of his mind for some recollection.

He had not read the Bible since he was a small boy, and had no especial inclination to start again. Like most energetic young men of the upper class, religion bored him stiff. "Why, I should have to say Lady Thrapston, I like the entire book too much to possibly select a favoured verse."

"A ridiculous answer, betraying further your impiety!" she snapped back. Bizarrely, her righteous anger was causing her to grip his back more tightly, rather than less. Hemsbridge feared that she had clamped herself to him so hard that he would not be able to flee without employing tactics better kept for a gentlemen's wrestling match; something he feared would not go down all that well in polite Somerset society.

"It appears that Somerset is nothing more than a den of godless vipers! If I do not find a good Christian man presently, my return trip to Northamptonshire will have to be brought forward!" and then Hemsbridge was saved. A perfect excuse to leave had just come skulking into the ballroom, in the form of his sometime friend and many-time rival Braydon Aldercott.

"You will excuse me my lady..." he said, as politely as he could manage. "Just such a man of virtue and piety has just entered the room, and I am obliged to convey to him my best wishes. You will excuse me." Lady Thrapston looked neither sad nor relieved as he left her, but retained the same expression of anger she had had all along.

"Hemsbridge" said Aldercott as he approached, in the ironic tone of a serial rogue and seducer.

"Aldercott" was all Hemsbridge needed to say in response. They knew each other well enough to dispense with formality, nodding and shaking hands lightly.

"What the devil have you been doing with yourself?"

"I was availing myself of some of the local entertainments," said Aldercott, smirking in his perverse way. "... and by golly were they entertaining."

"Oh yes, indeed?" said Hemsbridge. "Where exactly were you indulging in these 'entertainments'?"

"Why out in the grounds, with the prettiest wee hussy you've ever laid your eyes on. Far better than any of the dogs and dullards you see assembled around this ballroom." He gestured at the rather boring and unimpressive selection of women Hemsbridge had just now been trying his best to navigate.

"That I can believe. Who was she?"

"Her" said Aldercott, angling his head discreetly in the direction of a woman Hemsbridge immediately recognized. She was the exact same woman who had caught his attention before, and now she seemed even more radiantly beautiful. He noticed that she wore a diamond choker, close and tight about her neck, shimmering along with her pearly earrings and the diamond decorations scattered through her rich blonde hair.

He was captivated, but not just by her good looks. It seemed to him that she also had a wryness about her, an awareness of the world and a force of life that was instantly, unconsciously powerful. Compared to the insipid girls he had been forced to speak to, and dance with, she positively shone. This, coupled with the knowledge that she had already been engaged in an intimacy that Aldercott, jaded as he was, was willing to describe as 'very entertaining' was enough to get his mind moving rapidly towards the idea of becoming better acquainted with her.

"Lady Duckington" Aldercott continued. "Married, but you wouldn't know it - easier and filthier than a barracks room whore.

A lot of fellows I know have had their fill of her, Bellham amongst them."

"Bellham fraternized with her?" Hemsbridge queried, briefly shocked and dragging his eyes away from Lady Duckington for the first time in what felt like hours, but can only have been seconds.

Seemingly beyond his control, his eyes drifted back, to follow her progress through the room.

"Oh yes, they were quite a pair for a short while, her matrimonial status notwithstanding. That is, until he decided to run off and marry a serving girl 'for love', or whatever other damn fool excuse he's cooked up since. Duckington over there has been around the block a few times, let me tell you."

"What on Earth can you two fellows be gossiping about?" said Lady Hemsbridge, bustling over to the pair of them in a manner that suggested she had availed herself somewhat enthusiastically of the Duke of Whitehaven's excellent ratafia.

"What is there to discuss, when there are so many fine young ladies here, just waiting for eligible bachelors, such as yourselves, to sweep them off their feet and tuck a wedding ring onto their finger?"

"I dare say, mother, that I have the right to a private conservation with an old friend." Hemsbridge replied, impatient with his mother's insistence on constant attention to the marriage market.

"Pish, and I have the right to butt in, as and when I please, thank you very much! You wouldn't even be here if it wasn't for me."

She declined to mention whether she meant 'at the Duke of Whitehaven's ball' or 'on this earth' by the second remark.

"- and don't tell me you're both smitten with Lady Duckington now?" she continued, following both their eye-lines in the direction of the handsome young adulteress.

"The absurd predictability of men. I ask you! Show them a pretty face and a figure that suits an evening dress and they're off, like hounds after a scent. She may be fair, gentlemen, but she's no lady. A damned hussy if I ever saw one in all my life, and a nasty piece of work to boot."

She delivered this in an indiscreet mangle of words, too angry at the thought of him even looking at Lady Duckington to care who was listening. This, of course, only made Lady Duckington all the more fascinating. Sterling resolved to pursue her acquaintance at the earliest opportunity.

"Mother, I feel that the Duke of Whitehaven's steward may have been a little over-liberal when mixing the ratafia. You are rambling in a most improper manner, most unlike you." Hemsbridge threw Aldercott an embarrassed look, not that he'd ever much cared for the opinion of his drinking companion on familial matters.

"Stuff and nonsense. Never heard such a lot of Tommy-rot in all my life! I'm a Bassett by birth, need I remind you Sterling, long before I became a Hemsbridge, and we Bassetts have always been renowned for our ability to hold down our drink!"

"My dear Aldercott..." he said, turning with a wry smile to his companion, who had remained discreetly silent throughout his rather shameful exchange with his mother.

"I feel a round of cards might be in order. Shall we retire to the billiard room and leave my mother to find some rather less invigorating refreshment?"

"That sounds like a most excellent idea" replied Aldercott, grinning. 'Lead on.' The two men ignored the spluttering protestations of Lady Hemsbridge as they passed out of the room.

Chapter Three

Thoughts of Lady Duckington raced through Hemsbridge's mind all night. Try as he might, he could not seem to distract himself from her, her image seemed to be burned into the back of his retinas like a high midday sun he'd spent too long staring into. She was always there, seemingly, waiting for him, to draw his thoughts towards her, finding excuses to crop up in the obscure back passages of his mind.

Aldercott, after enough rounds of brandy and hands of cards, had been more than happy to dish the dirt. She'd had affairs left right and centre, in London townhouses and on country estates, with humble stable lads and with peers of the realm, rolled around in barrack rooms and haystacks and had nights of fragrant passion beneath the silk bedsheets of the rich and powerful. She was an *'insatiable harlot'* in Aldercott's now memorable phrase, who'd *'happily cop off with anyone with a bit of sense and a willingness for it.'*

He had been eager to find out more about her husband of course, but knew that it wouldn't do to seem too eager.

He had steered their conversation towards the topic lightly, and let Aldercott do the rest.

"Of course I'm not worried about her husband, old boy" he'd finally blurted, after yet another stiff mouthful of French brandy.

"He's an old fool and everyone knows it. Biggest moron in Berkshire I hear. There's an old story that goes around about him, people say he once spent three hundred guineas on a prize racehorse before he'd even had the chance to see it run. Went round all the counties, and all the courses in the land bragging about it, ordered it through an Indian merchant in London from the near East, said he was going to be the finest runner in England. Only what should happen when the damned horse shows up at his stable, eh? Turns out it's a bloody mare! And a short fat, dumpy one with little chubby legs to boot! Ha ha! Had I only been there to see the look on his face! All she was good for was breeding, and not racehorses mind! Carthorses at best! Ha!"

"I wouldn't be the first fellow to wager that's why he married Amelia, see..." Aldercott continued, blurting out Lady Duckington's first name in his drunken state.

"Spent a fortune on a useless, dumpy racehorse, so now he spends a fortune on a pretty, fine-figured wife! Ha ha! She can't stand him and he knows it, but at least he gets to share his bed with her, on the rare occasion she isn't yomping off with some other fellow that is!"

"So it wasn't difficult then?" asked Hemsbridge, considerably more sober than his caddish friend and keen to extract information.

"What wasn't difficult old boy?" Aldercott replied "- do spell it out for me, I've never been the brightest as well you know."

"You know perfectly well what I mean, Aldercott" Hemsbridge said "- setting your little assignation, with Lady D?"

"That? Oh not difficult at all! Easiest damn thing I've ever done in my life as it happens. Bit of chit-chat, bit of dancing, she was open as a Turkish whorehouse on a steamy June night. Squealed a bit as well, when I stuck it in her. Damned fine stuff."

And at that point, Hemsbridge had thought it best to change the subject...

*

Despite the revelations he'd gleaned from Aldercott, he was still thinking about Lady Duckington when he got up the next morning. What was she really like, this woman, this mirage, this fantasy figure on the edge of his life, who couldn't stay out of his head?

What was it that made her so open, so easy-going, so adventurous, when away from her marriage bed? He had no idea, but something about her fascinated him. He had to hear more, and then find her.

"I know the type" said his mother, soaking a slice of bread into her third boiled egg of the morning. A servant watched on mournfully, guessing that he'd have to make her another.

"Women generally can tell that sort of woman. Men have no eye for it whatsoever, fall for them, get up to all sorts of immodest silliness with them, realise their error too late. She's a hussy, Sterling, a Jezebel. She'd be better off in some sultan's harem somewhere - that way at least she could be paid to satiate her outsized appetite. She's best left well alone."

Lady Hemsbridge said this with a dismissive confidence, as she captured, just in time, the egg yolk that would otherwise have run, thick and golden, down her chin and onto her napkin.

"If you say so mother" said Hemsbridge, not allowing himself to betray the fact that he was only more intrigued by all of the hostility Lady Duckington seemed to attract from all quarters. To hear some people talk, he thought, you'd think she'd murdered the king himself.

"I mean, if I'm being absolutely charitable..." she continued, taking another large swallow of tea. In the absence of strangers, his mother was prone to indulging at breakfast.

"... I suppose one can't really blame a woman of her age, and..." Lady Hemsbridge paused to consider the next word. It was a rather delicate matter for her, "... and her certain, ah.... physical gifts, one can concede her those..." Hemsbridge nodded gravely. Even a gossip like his mother had to admit that Lady Duckington was quite a beauty.

"... then you could say that you can't entirely blame her for exploring extracurricular options, married, as she is, to a man nearly four times her age, who'll never produce any children."

Sterling's ear pricked up at this last bit. No children? And an aged husband?

That suggested there might be change afoot in the Duckington future, if only a potential suitor could hold out for the inevitable...

"All that said, there's absolutely no need for her to be so open about it! Why, there's nothing wrong with letting off a little steam, provided one doesn't generate scandal! Dash it all, the nobility of England could quite do without young ladies like her, generating stories for Fleet Street hacks to pick over and print in their rags! It's neither proper, nor decent!"

"Yes mother" said Sterling, barely paying any attention, his mind already considering the implications of her words. "Yes indeed."

Sterling repressed a sigh - another ball, another opportunity for Lady Hemsbridge to lecture her prodigal son on the importance of finding the right match.

They were in the carriage, driving up to Gloucestershire for the Earl of Stroud's *'little occasion'*, as it had been advertised on the invitations, Hemsbridge was forced to listen to a very long speech on the subject, forced to turn his head away from the family coat of arms and instead admire the pleasant West Country scenery.

Rolling hills, red-brick dairy farms, and the occasional sandy gorge all exerted far less pressure on him than that old image of the rampant lion and goat coming together over a shield embossed with a star and oak tree, symbols of the Hemsbridge line, a visual admonition to produce heirs and live up to traditions.

"You simply must produce an heir Sterling. There's no getting away from it" his mother said, as if speaking on behalf of the coat of arms itself.

"Can't you just settle for a nice girl with a good family? You don't want to be lonely all your life, chasing after strumpets after your looks have faded, your feet won't dance and all you think about during a conversation is how much you need the lavatory! Why my nanny always said, growing up, the only thing worse than an aged bachelor is an aged maid. Men grow old better than women it's true, but not much better, and you must look to the future, Sterling."

"Of course, mother." Hemsbridge muttered in reply. "I can do little else, as the subject appears to be the sole preoccupation of your mind, and the only topic you consider worth conversing on."

"Oh do be quiet boy!" she replied, in a matronly tone that made him glad none of his drinking companions was present to see him be chastised by his mother. "*My* sole intention is to do what's best for you, and for the family, that is all. You'll see, once we get to Hamblee House, there should be plenty of very nice and very eligible young ladies there, for you to convince yourself you've *'fallen in love with'*, whatever that's even supposed to mean, and then you can get on with the important business of producing heirs. That's what manners, when all is said and done."

"Yes mother" Sterling reluctantly agreed. "Whatever you say."

*

Any intentions Hemsbridge might have had, of following his mother's advice, were cast aside the moment they arrived at the ball, for the very first person that he saw, after being announced to the room by a footman and bowing obligingly to his hosts, was the woman who had stalked his dreams the past few nights, Lady Amelia Duckington. She was wearing a forest-green dress that his mother might have charitably described as 'slim-fitting'.

As far as most of the envious women onlookers were concerned, she was dressed like a cheap tart, a strumpet, a Parisian wench who might speak well but had the morals of a common tavern-whore. Nevertheless, with her golden-blonde hair, in a tight bun, and her slender figure, accentuated by the unusual French tailoring, she was a picture most of the men in the room were more than pleased to look at, all night long, even over the shoulders of their wives, or rather more coy dance partners.

Hemsbridge knew, at once, that he simply had to meet her at last, to dance and converse with her, and maybe..... but no, the thought was improper, but that did not stop him from having it, enjoying it even.... maybe taking her outside, out to the bushes...

First, though, he had to get through a conversation with his host, Lord Stroud, who was the size of a prize county hog in mating season, and a shade of red that matched the claret that he had been drinking all afternoon.

"I say old boy!" he roared, in a voice that would have been loud in central London but was positively booming by Gloucestershire standards.

"Haven't seen you since you were knee high to a pixie, eh what?! Ha ha! How you've grown!" at this point, Lord Stroud saw fit to slap Hemsbridge on the back with all the force of a heavy cavalry charge.

"D'you hunt at all m'boy? We shall simply have to have you up here for a jaunt, wonderful country for it, eh, what? I hear Edward IV used to ride around here, chasing hare and hound, though I dare say the topology's altered a little since, eh what?! Ha ha!"

"Yes, yes, I should imagine so, My Lord." Hemsbridge replied, softly. Lord Stroud could immediately tell that his attention was elsewhere, specifically directed at Lady Duckington, who no red-blooded man could help but classify as the prettiest woman in the room.

"Ah, but I can see you're distracted! Quite reasonable old boy, oh yes, she's quite a picture isn't she?" Lord Stroud's tone had shifted entirely, from manly affability to hungry lust. He took a great gulp of red wine and allowed a small amount of it to run down his chin. He was an old-fashioned sort of an aristocrat, the sort who cares more for feasting than public service, and knows his wealth and title can paper over any indiscretion. No-one was going to tell him off for spilling wine at his own ball, and he knew it.

"Lady Duckington. Fairest married woman in all of England. What I wouldn't give to be twenty years younger old boy! But, ah well, we oldsters must live on through the exploits of the young. Come, she's just finishing up with her present partner, I shall introduce you..."

Seeing that Lady Duckington was just at that moment unclasping her hands from the rather desperate grip of a pale, thin young fellow, whom Hemsbridge vaguely recognised from previous occasions of this sort, they set off to intercept her before any other eligible young bachelors could get in the way. Moments later, Hemsbridge's rather lugubrious host was presenting him, at last, to the object of his desires.

"Lady Duckington, have you had the honour of making the acquaintance of young Hemsbridge here?" She glanced at him noncommittally, as if waiting for something about her new acquaintance to spring up and grab her attention.

"I believe not, my lord" she said, her voice like the sensual touch of a silk scarf, smooth and light.

"Then might I take it upon myself to present him to you, and you to him, Marquess Hemsbridge, Lady Duckington."

"Charmed" Lady Duckington said, with the barest hint of a flirtatious giggle.

 She held out her hand to be kissed, with the easy grace of a woman who is used to being showered with attention from attractive young gentlemen. Hemsbridge stooped to kiss her, lingering on the moment, hoping to catch her eye as his lips met the soft whiteness of her glove, where it lay across her undoubtedly equally soft skin. She did not return the gesture

"... and now I shall leave the two of you to converse. I expect two fine young persons such as you have no desire to have an old boor like me loitering on the edge of the conversation, you will excuse me."

Lord Stroud left, rather indiscreetly, just as the swelling warmth of passionate desire started to heat Hemsbridge's lower body.

"I have heard your name mentioned in passing, Lady Duckington, at other balls in the county of Somerset. I believe we may have shared a ballroom, on at least one occasion, though I cannot recollect any words passing between us?"

"No indeed, my Lord" she spoke snappily, as if already bored with him, before they had even started to get to know each other.

Hemsbridge was experienced enough at this sort of thing to know that it was a flirtatious act, designed to sustain his interest, but he felt it more acutely with Lady Duckington, somehow. It was as if she had implanted herself in his head already, as if she was his in some way, and the thought of any other outcome was simply impossible to accept. Any hint that she might reject his attentions was making him anxious.

"I do not believe I have had such a pleasure. Are you here alone?"

"No, pray, I came up with my mother, from Somerset."

"With your mother?" she chose to mock him, her tone made that quite clear. He was, perhaps, a little old to be unmarried and traipsing after his mother to balls, and she made him feel it.

"Well I shall best be on my very best behaviour then…" she drew out every syllable, with a playful vivacity that aroused him greatly once again.

"But tell me my Lady" Hemsbridge continued, undeterred "- what brings a married Lady of distinction and respectability to an occasion such as this? Why, you cannot possibly be old enough to have children to chaperone in hopes of them making a good match, for your beauty is undimmed and your evening dress of such fine elegance that I am certain you have made most of the women here positively envious."

"Sir aims for flattery, but strikes sycophancy" she said, smoothing her dress down over her slender curves as she drew his attention to her body. It was pert and feminine in the French-cut dress, and Hemsbridge longed to wrap himself in it, to feel her body against his, skin to skin. He had been dreaming of this woman for a week, and he found his body more than ready to explore her in real life. His arousal was making his breeches rather uncomfortable, if truth be told.

"- but I think I can probably forgive you. After all, it takes little to impress, when the only comparison is the frumpy maids one sees at occasions like this. I mean, look at her" she pointed at a very plain looking girl, stumbling through a conversation with a friend in the corner "- she looks like she was dressed by her farrier for God's sake! And what hair! Barely fit to mop a floor with."

Hemsbridge tried to be discreet as his eyes examined the girl she commented on – it would not be the thing to be seen to stare. She was not inaccurate in her description of the girl, but not kind either.

"Uncharitable remarks, if not far from the truth."

"You will find me full of insight."

"Really? Insight for example, into what special attractions can lure a woman away from her matrimonial bed to take in a Gloucestershire ball?" Lady Duckington leaned in towards Hemsbridge. He could smell a distinct fragrance on her, sensual and over-powering, and almost feel the gentle heaving of her décolletage as she came closer. He knew that his breeches bulged, and that she was very aware of it, as she brushed against him.

"There are certain things I've had to search very long, and very hard, to find, with little success, in a wedding bed with a man of advancing years. They are better sought in the company of the young, and vigorous."

"Is that so?" as Hemsbridge spoke, he could feel his breathing growing faster, his heat beating out a rough tattoo as this scandalous woman gently rubbed his erect member through his tight-fitting cream breeches. It was intoxicating! And dangerous! And entirely wrong! But he wanted it to continue, he wanted to get closer to this woman in every sense, perhaps to do as so many other young men at balls were reputed to have done to her...

"Lady Duckington..." he continued, only just maintaining an appropriate degree of composure. "Considering our present physical proximity, and the convenient choice of the musicians, might I propose that we waltz?"

"I thought my Lord would never deign to ask!" she said, pulling away suddenly, and smiling for the first time in their brief, but dramatic conversation. "I suppose that, as we are now acquainted, we might as well take a moment to consummate our new-found intercourse, before all and sundry."

She stepped back, waiting for him to play the man and offer his arm. Gripping it with a confidence he had never before found in women at balls, Hemsbridge led her to the floor, swung her into his arms and took her by hand, as his other hand settled as low on her waist as was possible, without complete impropriety.

Adjusting to the melody of the orchestra at the far end of the room, he led her smoothly into the newly fashionable Viennese dance, with all the polish that he could manage.

Hemsbridge was not a perfectionist master of dance, but he could manage a decent waltz. Gliding sensuously around the floor, with such a sumptuous woman held close against him, he could suddenly see why many of the older generation might disapprove of this continental fashion.

With his waist so close to hers, and their legs sliding past one another's like courting swans, he felt the bodily closeness to her intensely. It sent a tingling down his spine, and though his midriff, down into his manhood.

The pressure of his tight breeches against his arousal was an exquisite torture as they moved – one which he was quite certain she was choosing to accentuate. He was ready for her, and she might as well have had him on a leash.

"You dance well enough, my Lord Hemsbridge" she hissed into his ear, with an almost aggressive sexuality.

"As do you, My Lady" he replied. "Tell me, is it this sort of vigorous stimulation that causes you to seek the company of men younger than your husband?"

The music carried them along, the swirling turns almost dizzying, and they made a sweeping turn, balanced and secure in each other's arms. They were a handsome pair, holding the attention of most onlookers, but so focussed on each other that they did not notice the attention. "… Or had you something else in mind?"

"My Lord is not far from the mark" she said, arching her spine in one languid movement towards him, intensifying the position of the dance.

"Although, I tend to find that it is away from the prying gaze of strangers that young men most effectively demonstrate their particular talents." Her piercing blue-violet eyes cut right through him. Compared to the insipid young things that he had been expected to consider for a wife, she was intoxicatingly vibrant, exotic and dangerous. He was completely captivated by her, longing to be with her, to satisfy himself in her arms.

"Lady Duckington" he said, smiling suggestively. "I must confess, all of this physical stimulation has quite warmed me, might I suggest a brief respite in the gardens?"

She raised her eyebrows at him, and smirked. She knew what he meant, but she was too clever to be so easily led. Pressing herself close to him, so that the soft expanse of her bosom met his hammering heart, she whispered a reply.

"I think not, on this occasion my Lord" he was stunned. Failure! Rejection! He paused, struck harder by the refusal than he could ever have thought possible. Then, as he was about to pull away, to run off and seek solace in the arms of some other, more straightforward girl, she surprised him.

"I would prefer it if we could continue our correspondence elsewhere. I have a modest townhouse in London, just off Bond Street. It's a quiet little den, why not pop up on the 14th? I don't believe there are any social engagements scheduled in the Somerset season around then?"

Hemsbridge steadied himself, holding back a sigh of relief. It would not do to let her see just how relieved he was, or how joyous he felt at her suggestion. He suspected that, should he do so, she would use the knowledge to tease him, to play with him, just to arouse him further.

But he was overjoyed - it was going somewhere after all! This dalliance had not been for nought! He knew enough to know that composure is almost always more attractive in a man than overt displays of emotion, at least in public!

"My Lady is most generous in her offer. I shall certainly consider it, and respond forthwith."

"Good boy" she responded, with a cheeky smile and a slight pinch of the Marquess' firm buttocks, as the dance ended and she slid her hands down his body provocatively, as they drew apart. That gesture was all he needed, to know that this had, for once, been a successful night at a ball.

*

That was not his mother's opinion of things, a fact which she made abundantly clear to him later. But even a lecture from his mother could not diminish his satisfaction with the evening. He simply bore with it, smiled and nodded in all the right places, and ignored every word that she said.

His mother was deeply unimpressed, and told him so. For once he did not care.

For the next three days, all that Hemsbridge could think about was Lady Duckington.

She was there, at the forefront of his mind, before he went to sleep, and as he woke up, his first thought.

She started appearing in his soup, her reflection caught in mirrors and on the reflective surfaces of the family silver. He lusted after her, and could not yet tell what the power of his feelings indicated.

Hemsbridge stared into the mirror as he contemplated this question. He was a handsome man, and there no denying it. He had strong features, well-articulated and clear.

His nose was straight, his lips were full, he had a square jaw and a full head of rich red-brown hair.

His eyes were an intense green, fresh as the day he'd first come into this world, but since then his experiences with women had given them a glint that the fairer sex found attractive. He had a complexity to him that they could immediately perceive, he was mostly a self-confident soul, yet he yearned for love, and in that area, his confidence was not so strong.

Was this love, what he felt for Lady Duckington? He could not possibly tell. She was certainly in his mind all the time, teasing and tormenting him, and there was no questioning his physical attraction to her.

A part of him feared that that was all that this was; that he was jealous of his oaf of a friend, Aldercott, and wanted to have this pretty young adulteress to himself.

There was also that - her married status. It loomed over her like a storm cloud, but it was also thrilling. She was married, she was known for her infidelities, she was a bored, forthright, highly-sexed woman who knew what she wanted from men.

Hemsbridge had never met anyone like her, and that was as terrifying as it was electrifying. He did not know what to think, but he knew for certain that he would go to her townhouse in London on the fourteenth.

Her footman had delivered a note, which he now studied. It was not the first time he had scoured her words for greater meaning, searched for any hidden depth that they might contain, and it would likely not be the last. Pacing casually over to the dressing table, he now retrieved the note, and regarded its written contents once more.

Sir, it began simply

I trust this correspondence finds you well, and that the Somerset season has not depleted your energies too severely, for I must confess a desire to make good on my promise of further confraternity. I enjoyed our brief encounter at Lord Stroud's gathering in Gloucestershire and I am led to believe, by the sentiments you expressed, and certain inferences from your manner and bearing, that you felt likewise. Considering that, I would be most honoured if you would join me for light refreshment and a continuation of our intercourse here in London on the fourteenth of June.

The house can be found at Number 42, Burton Lane, London, proximate to Bond Street, as I believe I may have mentioned at the ball. I should expect a cultivated gentleman of your self-evident qualities to be familiar with its location, but I suspect that if you are not, the footmen of the west end will know the locality well enough to be obliging in that regard. I would counsel against bringing any companions, least of all your darling mother. Lord Duckington will not be in attendance and I do not like to encourage congestion in my drawing room, when it is not required of me by the demands of my position in society. I am sure you understand, you didn't strike me as a fool.

I await your reply with interest.

Yours sincerely,

Lady Duckington

Hemsbridge had never received a more fascinating letter in all his life. It was positively dripping with suggestion and inference, even before one reached the final sentence of the second section. He felt like her plaything, as if she were a cat baring its claws and he a small animal for her to toy with. It was not a familiar sensation, but he found he enjoyed it. She would find that he had claws too – he wondered if she would enjoy that as much.

That she was insisting that he not bring his mother, and making it abundantly clear that, as she said, Lord Duckington would *'not be in attendance'*, he could not help but feel an excitement swell deep within him, spreading from his forehead, sweating in anticipation, down to his quivering toes, by the not inconsiderable route of his manhood. He was, as she had so boldly asserted, no fool, and he knew as any red-blooded male of a little experience and some feeling for carnal matters, what message she had intended to convey.

He was heading for a night of sensual pleasure in London, and he couldn't be happier about it.

*

But, first, he must endure another ball, and yet more lectures from his mother on the importance of finding the right match.

"Keep your eyes on the unwed ones Sterling!" she snapped at him, noticing that he was admiring the rather ample cleavage of Viscount Pelham's wife-to-be.

"There's no use expending unnecessary energy on those who are already betrothed, or worse, wed!" at this last word, thoughts of Lady Duckington rushed at Hemsbridge, causing him to physically wince, awaiting his mother's next words.

He took another sip of port and pretended that nothing had happened.

"Sorry mother" he said, hoping to mollify her for now.

"I'm afraid sometimes one's masculine instincts can get the better of one." He stole another glance at the other man's pretty fiancée, realised that he was indeed, wasting his time and behaving in an improper fashion, and gave up.

"And of what of your dynastic instincts, hmm? Your family, your successors, your name, Sterling? It'll only die out if you go chasing after shapely shadows, don't you know?"

"You are as ever, abundantly correct, mother" he replied. He had, by now, given up on attempting to make any counter-argument. He knew that she would only grind him down with her stubborn commitment to her noble family's values.

The only problem on this occasion, as at so many others he had attended in Somerset society, was that there no-one of any interest to him there. As the piano plonked from sombre introductions to encouraging swirling waltzes on the dance floor, he could only look on in disappointment at the succession of plain, dull, immature women that he was expected to try and flirt with.

"I mean, I suppose you could always go the same way as our host" Lady Hemsbridge said, with a laugh.

"Consigning his fortune to perdition, and giving half of his fine selection of residences to some serving girl who happened to have spilled jellies down his front in a manner he found inexplicably stimulating! I ask you, is that a legitimate way of finding a bride, Sterling?"

Sterling had not the heart to point out to her that their host, an old companion of his, Richard Maitland, now Viscount Bellham, owner of this fine townhouse close to the river in Chelsea, was at that very moment, standing right behind her.

"Lady Hemsbridge, you will excuse my interjection…" the yelp that she narrowly managed to suppress caused both of the young men to share a smile and a discreet chuckle. Bellham was a modest and good-humoured fellow, who did not mind being the subject of old ladies gossip. Indeed, one might have quipped, in marrying a serving girl for love, he had positively invited such things. Hemsbridge spotted the girl he had married, twirling around the drawing room, playing the hostess with an easy grace that defied her humble origins, in a gorgeous gown of a delicate apricot shade that set of her rich dark red toned hair, and envied Maitland for having successfully made one girl immeasurably happy.

"I trust that the two of you are enjoying our modest occasion here in Chelsea…"

"Oh yes! Absolutely My Lord! Marvellous!" Maitland could barely finish his sentence before Lady Hemsbridge had interrupted. In her desperation to atone for her inappropriate comments about her host, within his hearing, she was trying rather too hard to be polite.

"Wonderful. The décor is, I'm afraid, a little drab for my tastes. I prefer the subtle elegance that has recently come into fashion in the West End, though I suppose this ballroom is pleasant enough."

"Indeed it is sir!" declared Lady Hemsbridge, her eyes wide with excitement.

She gestured sweepingly, taking in the whole room, from the high windows on the back wall to the austere family portraits which lined the side, via the vast crystal chandelier that hung over their heads.

"And, in fact, I rather think that it becomes you better to remain rooted in longer established fashions. Why, if all of us exclusively followed the latest fads and newest styles, then none of us would have any energy, money, or indeed, good sense left over! Sometimes the old ways are the best, even if you young gentlemen don't believe it to be so."

"I er, er, er, find that I quite agree with your sentiments, my er, lady" interjected a newcomer, whom neither Lady Hemsbridge nor her esteemed son had ever encountered before.

"You are quite right. Without the, er, er inheritance of previous generations' expertise and good labours, we would all er, be quite lost! Traditions, like great houses, must er, er, persist, what?"

Lady Hemsbridge eyed the new arrival curiously. He was a slim man, and rather tall, with a hooked nose and slightly beady eyes that looked like they'd spent a little too much time peering into obscure books. He wore a brass pince-nez and unfashionable clothes, but he had a full head of dark hair, and the air of a man who had once been handsome, without even realising it. Lady Hemsbridge could not help but be quite taken with him.

"My apologies my Lady, I do not believe that the two of you have been introduced..." Bellham cut in rather smoothly, fixing the cuffs of his bottle green dress coat in a single movement.

"May I present to you Professor Edward Greenidge, of the Royal College of Arms, a most learned fellow, and, as the researcher who demonstrated my wife's noble inheritance, the man to whom I am more grateful than anyone else on earth."

"My Lord is most er, gracious in his praises. My achievement was quite incidental, you must understand, though I er, er accept the compliment graciously."

"Why…" said Lady Hemsbridge, growing more fascinated by the man

"…. Greenidge? Sir, are you perchance, the son of Viscount and Lady Camberton, late of the county of Somerset?"

"The very same" he said with a resigned, scholarly air. "Alas, I am all that remains of my immediate family, save my brother Reginald, the current Viscount, who is not of good health. I devote myself now whole-heartedly to er, er my studies. But tell me, er, my lady, how have you come by er, er, such a great knowledge of er, er, the great houses of England as to identify me so swiftly? Few these days have heard of er, my family, as we have not prospered so much in recent generations, and our estates are small…"

"Well, I may not be a scholar of the College of Arms, my good Mr. Greenidge, but I am something of an enthusiastic amateur in questions of family history, if you would not think it impudent of me to make such a boast."

"Indeed not, My Lady!" Greenidge almost bounced on the spot at this news. At last, someone who shared his passion! And a lady to boot, of, he suspected, a similar age to himself, but still distinctly charming with her youthful beauty not completely faded!

Before he could say anything further, she was enthusiastically asking questions of him, seeking to plumb his great depths of knowledge.

"Now tell me Mr. Greenidge, for I've always been concerned to know more, the House of d'Allemberd...." She took him by the arm and led him away from her son and host, leaving the two younger men to exchange a knowing grin, and a shrug of surprise.

"I suppose we'd best leave them to it, Sterling" Bellham whispered.

"Yes, Richard" Hemsbridge replied. "I suppose so. I am grateful – my mother needs something to focus on, other than my unwed state!"

Richard grinned at him, clapped him on the shoulder with a laugh, and went to see to his other guests.

Chapter Six

Lady Duckington awaited Hemsbridge's arrival with considerable interest. She had not been lying in her letter. She was keen to see him, to seize this opportunity. Her husband was away, down on the Sussex coast to see one of the few remaining among his friends who hadn't yet died. She had been surprised that he would undertake the journey, as he was somewhat frail and had not been well of late, but she hoped that he would take his time about it.

She was glad, as ever, to get away from the old man, and gladder still that Lord Duckington had not decided to invite his old companion up to London to entertain him alongside her. All that their conversation seemed to consist of, was trying to recall the names of people who'd been dead for years, or complaining of the various illnesses and ailments they had suffered from. She was too young for that, too full of life. She needed other stimulations.

Hemsbridge might provide just such stimulation, she thought. He was handsome, energetic, around her age and unwed. Bachelors who had nearly reached their thirtieth year were the ideal candidates for adultery. They were more sensitive and practiced as lovers than their younger counterparts, but still had the enthusiasm of men in their earlier twenties.

They tended to approach encounters whole-heartedly, as if fearing this might be the last time they got to copulate outside of a marriage chamber. Lady Duckington instinctively understood men and their ways, what moved them and what filled them with dread. She had used this talent to her advantage over the last few years, but gained an unflattering reputation in the process.

Her brief conversation with Hemsbridge had been enough to stimulate her interest in him. The pair had danced together well, and enjoyed a flirtation that was as smooth as it was exciting. She rather regretted to recall – even wincing now at the thought of it, that he had seen her being rude about other women, which was poor form under any circumstances, but especially bad at a ball.

That evening she had also snapped at a footman who she had deemed to be standing too close to one of her conversations with another gentleman. She had drawn disapproving looks from other guests for this, something she dearly hoped Hemsbridge had not seen.

Amelia knew that, sometimes, her lust for life and pride in herself, her looks, her brains, her charms and her breeding, could get the better of her.

She was a woman who enjoyed attention and controversy, was given to strong opinions and harsh jokes, and so she often came across as unkind, or unfeeling. This was not truly her nature, yet many mistakenly saw these traits in her on first meeting, and so she had struggled to find lasting friends. She had become somewhat bitter about it, even as a girl, and had chosen to act as they believed her to be, rather than try to change their opinions.

She discovered that acting in such a way drew a crowd of 'friends' to her – not true friends, but a sycophantic collection of young women who were too afraid to have opinions of their own, but were willing to blindly follow hers. It was darkly amusing, but the comedy was wearing thin, ten years later.

As a younger woman, before her parents had seen fit to make a match for her with Lord Duckington, she had not been short of attention, at balls and other social events, from eligible and, in many cases, attractive, young men. And yet she had garnered no proposals, owing to her reputation as a discourteous scandal-monger. She looked down now into her tea and sighed a heavy sigh.

Deep down, Amelia feared that she could not love or be loved. She certainly knew herself and the habits of gentlemen well enough to know that she was attractive, indeed, any number of short-lived flings in country gardens, or pleasingly turgid breeches pressed against her frock as they held her close in a waltz, had confirmed as much. Women hated or envied her for her effect on their men. Men would perform for her like dancing monkeys if she wished them to, and would compete lightly with one another in their efforts to flirt.

But anything more serious, more rewarding than short, meaningless sessions of copulation (for she could not call them love-making) seemed somehow to elude her. It did not seem to be something that gentlemen saw in her. They valued her lithe body, her pretty face, perhaps even her open and vivacious manner, but they did not seem to want to get at her soul, or hear her thoughts on serious and substantial matters. As long as that remained the case, she would remain unsatisfied in affairs of the heart, tied to an ailing bored old husband and filling the emptiness by touring the shires looking for flighty young bucks to seduce.

She cast her mind back to her youth and there seemed to find the source of her haughtiness. Despite her evident prettiness, she had been a shy girl, and had worried greatly about everything, from the fortunes of the Duke of Wellington's armies in Spain, to the fact that her sister's hair seemed to be a prettier shade than hers. As a result, she had been retiring in society, and had used cruel humour and wicked remarks to her lessers as a way of showing strength. It was easy to seem important if you snapped at servants and laughed at people less pretty or privileged from behind their backs. It was a regrettable habit, but an understandable one.

It had taken her rather a long time to realise that, and to understand what she did, and why, at all. But she had had years to think, to watch how men and women responded to her, and to reach the point where she could no longer ignore the truth. She had brought this situation upon herself, through her own actions. There were no options. She had to live with what she had created, no matter what she truly wanted, or needed.

And what she needed was a man. That much seemed clear - a real man that is, not some wealthy old duffer to provide her with dresses and cream teas, or some pleasant young milksop who would shower her with affection but give her nothing real, but a man. A strong man, a rough man, even, a man to stand up for her, fight for her, carry her away from her anxieties and into a brighter future on his broad, broad shoulders - someone who could make it possible, just a little, for her not to have to be strong, in the face of others opinions. She pictured her ideal now.

He would be cocky, a little arrogant even, in a way that was intriguing without being overbearing. He would have humour, and share it with male friends, but never at the exclusion of her, or at her expense. He would be wealthy and have good taste, yet neither of these would be the focus of his life. Rather than limply complimenting her and giving her things all the time, he would be sparing in his affections, but sincere in his love for her, showing that he really meant it. And above all, he would be handsome, and in good shape, not a fat, ailing, gout-ridden old man like Lord Duckington.

She laughed at herself, a cynical, self-deprecating laugh, for surely these were the fairy-tale dreams of a young miss, barely out of the schoolroom. But they were her dreams too. The images came to her, the strong arms, the powerful thighs, the lean muscular torso that could be hers every night once she tore away his dress coat and shirt. He would have brown hair, a firm jaw-line, a straight nose and piercing eyes that one could almost drink. He was, she thought with a fluttering gasp, more than a little like Sterling Asterwood, the Marquess of Hemsbridge.

Giggling, a little hysterically, at herself, Lady Duckington sat back down. She had not even realised that she had been up on her feet, but all this day-dreaming of the ideal man had filled her with a new burst of irresistible energy.

Coming back down to earth, she realised that she was wasting her time. Until her husband had passed, it wouldn't even matter if such a seemingly impossible man ever did come along – there would be nothing she could do to make him hers. And, despite his age and corpulence, and the ongoing series of minor ailments, the family physician did not foresee any serious issues for Lord Duckington at present.

She was stuck in her marriage for now, and might as well make the best of it.

But then, at that very moment, the doorbell rang, and changed everything…

Chapter Seven

Sterling Asterwood was no stranger to encounters with ladies. This time however, it felt different. The setting was strange, it was true, as was the nature of their meeting. He had never before been summoned to a woman's house with so little pretext. It was obvious what was going to happen, and perhaps that was enough to stir an unfamiliar nervousness to accompany the more familiar feeling of increasing arousal.

He was excited, but apprehensive. Those would have been the words he'd use, had he been questioned, for whatever reason, on his present disposition. Travelling in the manner of a well-to-do tradesman rather than an out and out aristocrat, he had chosen to take a plain black hansom cab through the streets of West London, not wanting to draw attention to himself. Sitting in the somewhat grubby cab, with a plain brown coat covering his finely tailored and fashionable clothes, he felt a little odd.

He was used to taking alcohol before liaisons with the fairer sex, and to being around plenty of other young ladies and gentlemen. Almost all of his experience in this regard, outside the brothels of his youth, was of short and sudden affairs, the work of a single evening, carried out in a flush of passion, often in the open air. To be doing this so casually, so formally, so privately was all as good as alien to him.

He arrived at the door. It was sleek and stylish, like all of the surrounding residences, with the look of having had a new coat of glossy paint recently applied. Bizarrely, this small detail added to his nervousness. What if Lady Duckington, a woman whose presence at the back of his mind had only grown in the past few days, as he examined and re-examined the letter, pondered his feelings and speculated as to the course of this encounter, thought him coarse, or unfashionable? What if he was not sufficient to her high standards of taste and class?

He had money and breeding it was true, but he did not fit with London society well, its fashions and its mores having always seemed annoying to him, constraining, and deeply associated with his mother's attempts to find him a wife. He was considered odd by some of the ton – a Marquess who did not trade on his status, or look down on others. Albeit, his was a significant lineage, but not a long one, as a Marquessate – the King had rewarded his great grandfather with the higher title, for services rendered to the crown.

The same could not be said for Lady Duckington's husband, a true grandee, as his mother might have said – he might be but a Viscount, but his family history was long, and the title had been with them for many centuries.

He feared he might be beneath her, or that his affections would be rebuffed for some other, unknowable reason. Or, perhaps a knowable reason, one which had cost him the affections of ladies before.

He knocked briskly, and a butler answered the door - a short, swarthy man, with a very light Welsh accent that he couldn't quite hide.

"Lord Hemsbridge, I presume?" he said, drawing out the final syllable.

"Yes, yes that's me." Hemsbridge almost stuttered his response, having expected that he would have to explain himself rather more. Perhaps Lady Duckington's staff were used to facilitating this sort of meeting. The footman nodded and took his coat and hat, with barely a raised eyebrow at the disparity in quality between the outer coat and the exquisitely tailored clothing beneath.

"Do please come in, my Lord, My Lady awaits you in the Drawing Room. This way."

"Thank you..." Hemsbridge followed him through the grand entrance chamber, past a double-winged staircase, with an elegant wrought iron bannister standing above a sleek parquet floor. It was the sort of room his mother would have described as 'showy', but he rather liked it at once.

The Butler, with a discreet flourish, led him down a short corridor and into a drawing room at the back of the house that was as airy as it was inviting. Great yellow silk curtains hung around the edges of high windows, looking out on a well-maintained area of greenery in the garden.

Sitting before it, lounging on a crimson velvet chaise, with a set of bone china tea cups on a delicate small table in front of her, was Lady Duckington, looking as elegant and radiant as ever, in a rich gold, lace trimmed dress, which would not have been out of place in a ballroom.

"My Lord Hemsbridge" she said at once, putting him at ease with the confidence and sense of play in her voice. "It is good of you to have made the trip up to London." She glanced over his shoulder. The Butler was still standing dutifully by the door.

"You may leave us now, Jenkins" she said, tersely. With a polite nod, and what Hemsbridge almost saw as a wry smile directed at him, the Butler took his leave.

"Please, my Lord" Lady Duckington continued, after Jenkins had left them in peace. "- take a seat."

"Thank you." He leaned over and kissed Lady Duckington's hand, as he accepted her offer of a seat beside her on the chaise.

She seemed almost surprised that he had simply kissed her hand, rather than presuming to go straight to her lips and neck. He had, at least, some pretext of gentlemanly behaviour, she thought with satisfaction.

"You are aware I am sure, my Lord Hemsbridge, of what it is that has compelled me to summon you here to London?"

"I feel I have some notion, yes, my Lady."

"And you are aware as well I take it, that my husband is not present in the house?"

"You made that abundantly clear in your letter."

She eyed him, eyes sparkling devilishly, and for the first time Hemsbridge felt his slight discomfort disappear in the face of his arousal. He took her in, her intense blue violet eyes, her golden hair, her perfectly shaped body, and felt himself become hard, desire for her almost overriding all other thought.

"Then…" she continued, leaning towards him, stretching her neck and arching her back in a sensual movement.

"… I feel that, considering the tone of our earlier interactions, it would be quite fitting for me to do this." Before Hemsbridge had time to really fathom what was happening, she slid her hand to the back of his head and pulled him to her, with a force he had never before felt from a Lady, and kissed him with wanton passion.

He had not thought it possible to be more aroused than he was, but his body had a different opinion. His breeches became a most painful prison, and he felt compelled to return her kisses with equal vigour. Wrapping his strong arms around Lady Duckington, he gripped her tightly to him, feeling the contours of her body, as he had at the ball but a few nights hence. Their tongues collided with a singular energy, two conscious bodies pushing at each other as hard as they dared.

Hemsbridge was quite amazed! To think that the gloss of aristocratic nicety and formality, with servants and procedures, could be stripped away with such ease, and replaced with this raw sensuality – from a woman! He was quite aware of his own capacity for raw and somewhat aggressive passion, but this, from a woman, was a new experience.

The sensations he felt were not new to him, but they did have a new intensity, for being delivered in a context such as this, sober and unashamed, with time and space and privacy all assured, and with a woman of his own class, who, it appeared, wanted him for his own sake, for the pleasure that they might take in each other, rather than for his money.

He knew that he, himself, was always just a thin veneer of civility away from raw and aggressive passion – he worked hard to not frighten or overwhelm the women he had been with, but there were times when that slipped. It worried him. But perhaps, he hoped, this woman was different - he could feel the same raw need in her.

They relaxed into each other's arms, sharing the chaise, but their lust for each other quivered between them, like an invisible force that would not be denied. If anything, it grew in intensity, like the hull of a ship that has been breached, only for more water to stream in as the hole grows.

This image occurred to Lady Duckington and she could only think of her own womanhood, swelling in pulsating response to Hemsbridge's touch, his kiss, his passionate and inviting embrace. Her body tingled all over and she longed to be free of the layers of clothing that constrained her. There was only one thing to be done. She pushed him away with a light flirtatious laugh, rose to her feet, and offered her hand.

"Come, my Lord" she purred at him. "Let us continue proceedings in the bedchamber."

With his palm held firmly in her grasp, Hemsbridge followed.

Watching every step of her swaying feminine grace, he could feel himself growing harder still, until it was almost too much to bear. He had to have her now, to lose himself in her fine body and pleasure her, and himself, for all he was worth. Silently, with only a saucy turn of the head and a flickering smile, she led him up the stairs.

The click of the shutting door was all the provocation that Sterling needed, to express his overpowering lust. It was just too much. Taking a fraction of a moment to make sure that the door was, indeed, firmly shut, he reached for her. Grasping her buttocks firmly in one hand, to pull her against him, and cupping her face in the other, he kissed her with all the force of a stiff November gale. As he held her to him, pressing his bulging breeches against her delicious body, just for a moment, part of him was worried.

He knew that he had a habit of allowing his passions to run away with him, to lead him to an aggression in his love making which had resulted in him being rebuffed by ladies not used to the intensity of passion he so often felt when making love. It was an issue that had nagged at him for years, dogging otherwise promising encounters with women like Lady Charlotte back in Derbyshire. He could charm them, but then had an unfortunate tendency to overwhelm them once in private, to approach them much too aggressively for the gently bred ladies of the aristocracy to cope. Even the women of the brothels sometimes found him too much. Then such thoughts left him, for his need became too great, as she moved her body against him, intentionally inflaming his passion further.

Lady Duckington's passion appeared to equal his, she too seemed to be moved by strong arousal, to desire physical pleasure first and emotional intimacy later.

'Slow down for Gods' sake Sterling!' he could hear himself screaming in his head, in a voice that was half way between his own and his mother's. He seemed, almost, to have forgotten that he was in the presence of a Lady, and a guest in her house to boot, so intent was he on sating his desire, now, right away, rather than waiting and playing the gentleman as was proper.

'She's still here. She invited you here, and has made her feelings abundantly plain.' Coherent thought ended there - he could not stop now had he wanted to, his lustful tongue traced her lips and explored the cavern of her mouth, he ran his hands over her shapely buttocks and bosom, then grasped her hard in his arms and pulled her close.

He fought the desire to rip the dress from her, instead dragging the bodice down to expose her hardened nipples to his touch. He took first one, then the other, in his mouth, teasing them with licks and nips of his teeth, pleased at the little mewls of pleasure that she was making.

Somewhere deep in his mind, he realised that she was not pulling back in any way. She did not seem alarmed or perturbed at his advances, in fact far from it. She was enjoying it. She liked his rough kissing, his firm grip, his wandering hands. She was not some maid in a stately garden determined to keep him at bay, but a full grown woman, hungry for a man's touch. That awareness freed him of any last constraint.

His hand slid lower, over her hip and down.

He found his way around her petticoats, feeling the smoothness of her skin and her shapely frame. His fingers explored, and, discovering that she wore no drawers, came to rest on her most intimate place. She did not recoil or shriek; rather she let out a low gasp of encouragement, of pleasure. He could not only hear that she was enjoying his advancing physical closeness, but feel it as well, in the soft, moist area beneath her clothes. He rubbed there now, finding exactly the right spot, at first gently, but then with greater vigour, drawing more low groans from her.

Grasping with his hands and nibbling at her neck and breasts with his tongue and teeth, he had the clear sense that his harsh advances were welcome, that, indeed, they seemed to be precisely what his partner wanted. The recognition of that was enough to tip him, again, completely out of thinking, and into lust fuelled action.

He lifted her, as if in a blur, in a single, smooth movement, captivated by her passion, her presence, and carried her, in a few short strides, from the doorway to the bed.

He pushed her down, and firmly rolled her over, holding her down, his hands undoing the laces of her dress and stays with desperate urgency, as he pressed himself hard against her delicious rounded buttocks, and kissed her neck and shoulders and he drew the gown down. The lacing all undone, he lifted off her for a moment, and she turned, lightning fast, and, in an instant, her hands were grappling with his breeches.

The dress had fallen completely to her waist, and her beautiful breasts were exposed to his touch. Ignoring that completely, she freed his cock from his breeches, her hands sliding over its hard, straight length.

Leaning down, she lapped at his hardened tip with her tongue, and then very deliberately took him into her mouth. Her head tilted up slightly, and her eyes were dancing as they met his. It was obvious that she was revelling in his gasps of pleasure as much as he had enjoyed hers.

Sterling moaned as Lady Duckington took him deeper into her mouth, finding that he was unable to prevent himself from thrusting into her in response. Her lips and tongue moved fluidly, changing tempo, switching angles, creating a sealed chamber exclusively for his enjoyment. His mind soared, and before he knew it he was transported to a higher plane of pleasure, as her actions tipped him over the edge.

He gasped as she released his member from her mouth's embrace. With an inviting smile, and their first moment of eye contact in what felt like an age, she stood to unselfconsciously draw her dress and chemise down, allowing them, and her unlaced stays, to fall in a tangle at her feet, then reclined back further on the bed, waiting to receive him. Eagerly he shed his disordered clothing to unveil his well-toned torso, his broad barrel chest and tightly tapered stomach muscles. His manhood jutted proudly, already hardening again at the sight of her naked body.

"I see you have developed your body well, my Lord Hemsbridge" she said sassily, running her tongue over her full lips. "I take it that you have spent many an hour on vigorous rides."

"Many" he assured her, his need surging at her words. "- though few quite as vigorous as this." He joined her on the bed, and, as he uttered the final word, their tongues and then their bodies, came together.

Her hands reached for him, but he captured them, pulling them above her head and holding them there, trapped in one of his. Her eyes lit with excitement, and she squirmed in his grasp, her body rising to meet his, as he thrust himself deep within her, in a single powerful movement.

She cried out in pleasure, and arched herself, her hips rising to meet him as he swiftly found a smooth rhythm and let all of his aggressive need drive his thrusts. They moved with one intent – driven by an overwhelming need to find completion. He held her tighter as the sensations grew more acute, gripping her, keeping her hands prisoned above her, and bent his head to kiss and nip at her breasts, and at her elegant neck. She pulled against him, but it was not in a wish to be released – more as a result of the need to move in response to the intensity of sensation, as she cried out her pleasure, and signalled her encouragement of his actions with kisses and nips of her own, to any part of him that she could reach, accompanied by moaning utterances from her throat.

"Oh yes, my Lord" she managed to pant "pray continue! Take me!" and he did as he was instructed, gripping her harder, subjecting her to his will, to his overwhelming, long repressed need, pinning her down and unleashing a barrage of pent-up sexual energy, energy which he had been saving up for years, but had never, until now, quite found the right partner to expend it on.

They reached their peak together, with such simultaneous intensity that they could not help but collapse in spent delight, pausing a moment to hold each other, as they considered what had just passed between them.

After some moments of silence, they both laughed and grinned at each other, their delight in the experience leading them to lay soft, affectionate kisses on one another as if to break the spell. The moment of bestial passion had passed. They were no longer animals but human once more. The beast within, which Hemsbridge had unleashed at Lady Duckington's insistence, was once more put on a leash. They rolled apart, and lay back on the rumpled bed, needing to catch their breath, both staring at the elegantly carved plaster of the ceiling, marvelling at what had just happened in this ordinary well-kept bedroom.

"You have quite reinvigorated me, Lord Hemsbridge" said Lady Duckington, bringing them both gliding gently back down to earth. "Why if I had any gift for poetry, I would say something to the effect of, *'your presence has been like a cool breeze on hot summer's day, refreshing and welcome indeed.'"*

"My Lady demonstrates her talents most ebulliently" He leant in to plant a delicate, nibbling kiss upon her ear "- in more ways than one, as well. But my Lady, after what has just passed between us, I must ask you to address me by my given name, which is Sterling, for surely we are rather past the need for formality in private!"

"Stuff!" said Lady Duckington. "I have but one talent and that is in the realm of love-making. You flatter me rather too eagerly, Sterling."

"Perhaps." He turned to her again, raising himself up on his elbow and considering her with a look that she could only interpret as an invitation to further love play. "- But I have a certain incentive to please you, do I not?" She did not speak in reply, but merely laughed lightly, and leaned in close to him so that they could do it all, all over again.

Chapter Eight

Amelia awoke to a deep sense of satisfaction, tingling all over her body. Hemsbridge had brought her exactly what she had hoped, and then politely left, with a courteous farewell. This was not a new arrangement; she had shared many such nights of passion with other attractive young gentlemen, and most had gone at least passably pleasantly, and then ended, discreetly.

This time however, a strange thought came to her, unexpectedly: maybe she'd like to do that again, with him.

It was not only that Hemsbridge had proved a gifted lover, sensitive to her needs, with considerably more intensity and fire to him than most of the young Lords she had dallied with, though this was certainly true. It was also that, despite all her better instincts, and for reasons she could not ever have properly explained even if she tried, she felt somehow drawn to him.

She was filled with tantalising sensations, whenever he entered her thoughts. Not since her early girlhood, well before she was wed to old Lord Duckington, had she felt anything like this way. She had been cynical about love for so long, written it off as the preserve solely of poets, lunatics and children, that she had nothing to measure these sensations by. Doubt was niggling at her and she was not at all sure of what this sensation may mean. Perhaps she was simply indulging in fantasies born of her increasing ennui with the gentlemen of the *ton*.

After running a hand down her smooth skin, still electric to the touch after last night's liaison, pleased that the sensations were still there, lapping at her like waves at low tide, she dragged her thoughts back to reality. She was a married woman. The ring on her finger confirmed that, reminded her of that, every day when it clicked against her cutlery and made certain manoeuvres of the hand uncomfortable or difficult. It was there to symbolise the vow that she had taken; 'till death us do part' and all the rest of it, the stuff that little girls dream of all day in their nurseries, and which mothers are so keen to encourage. The things that trapped her, irrevocably, as she was.

Even to consider that she might develop more feeling for Hemsbridge than the delights of a passing assignation or two was not only silly, it was wrong. It went against all social convention, against her duties as a wife and against the law of the land, not to mention God's law as well (not that she'd been too worried about him when she'd been on her back with her legs in the air and the Marquess of Hemsbridge deep inside her, she had to admit).

A married woman could pursue private affairs and occasional flings if she must, but emotional distance was the order of the day. Becoming attached to one of her occasional lovers would be beyond foolish.

Obviously, she was simply being enamoured of his passionate performance as a lover – which was beyond refreshing after the flat, and barely competent, hurried couplings that most men seemed to think were all that was required.

This did not mean though, she thought naughtily, that she could not see Lord Hemsbridge ever again. *'Oh no, Amelia'* she said to herself, almost winking at her own devilish reflection in her mother of pearl gilded hand mirror. *'There's absolutely nothing that says you can't do that.'*

She sprang out of bed in a single movement, compelled by the energy of these new feelings, and rang the bell for her maid. There was a ball tonight in Berkshire, just outside London, at the country estate of the Earl of Teverson.

She would go, dress her best, court attention, and if a certain Lord Hemsbridge was in attendance, see how the course of events ran. Chuckling to herself, she flung open the varnished oak doors of her wardrobe, and considered her options…

*

Hemsbridge was, indeed, in attendance at the ball.

His mother, who believed that he had passed the previous evening at his club, carousing with his gentleman friends, had absolutely insisted upon his attendance.

"Mother, I am quite worn out after last night's exertions," he had protested "- besides, is it truly plausible that missing one occasion in the society calendar is going to ruin my amorous chances for life?"

"It could, Sterling!" she had barked, tapping him on the wrist in a manner that suggested she had quite forgotten he was no longer an infant.

"It very well could! One can never truly know with these things; it is possible that the one ball you fail to attend is the one at which you would otherwise have met your perfect match; beautifully well-endowed with estates and fortune."

"And, I should hope, a charming personality and looks to my taste as well, mother?"

"Hmmph, if you insist, but if you ask me, you're looking at a gross misapplication of priorities - think of the family name and honour my boy! Those come first, remember?"

"Yes mother" he mumbled, "whatever you say."

And so he had gone and called for his valet, to assist him in dressing in his best cravat, and a rather fetching bottle green coat which he dimly remembered he had worn to that wedding reception in Derbyshire some time ago, and he set off, dutifully, but without much enthusiasm, for the ball.

*

Aldercott was there, of course.

Aldercott was often there, when Hemsbridge didn't want him around, bragging and sidling up to the prettiest young misses.

Though he had no desire to discuss it in the comradely, 'boys club' way Aldercott would inevitably favour, Hemsbridge just knew that Aldercott would raise the subject of Lady Duckington. With the predictability of a pocket watch, it was the first thing he said:

"Hemsbridge! Had a crack at Lady D yet?" Aldercott said, with all the subtlety of a volley of cannon.

"My dear Aldercott, so good to see you, as always" was all he could be bothered to say in reply.

"I'll take that as a yes then, old boy! Don't blush, it's quite natural, birds and the bees and all that, eh what? Quite a girl I must say, quite a girl."

"She's not really a girl, is she Aldercott?" Hemsbridge said, betraying his impatience. 'She is, I believe, twenty seven, and has been married for nigh on ten years!"

"Well no need to split hairs over small matters of biography!" spluttered Aldercott, helping himself to another generous serving of rum punch. "She looks like a girl, having retained plenty of her beauty, despite being married to an old codger! And she has the... energy... of a girl, when it comes to having it off, that I can tell you! Not that you need my opinion on the subject, eh?"

Aldercott winked, and slapped him on the arm so hard that there was an audible crack, drawing the attention of a few onlookers. Some rather plain looking girls tittered at the two handsome men in the corner, talking amicably, at least to their eyes. Hemsbridge ignored them. He was, quite simply, not in the mood for tedious conversation with debutantes.

"I heard from a few of the other chaps in attendance that she's set to show her face tonight!" Aldercott continued, between mouthfuls of punch. "Making the trip down from the little townhouse she and Lord Duckington have got in the west end. All the way out to Berkshire just for one night, no husband in tow! Bloody hell the gal's insatiable! You couldn't pay to keep her away!"

"I'm sure she has her reasons" Hemsbridge replied, trying desperately to think of some means of changing the subject. If Aldercott wheezed on like this all night, he might be forced to challenge him to a duel just to get him to shut his mouth for five minutes.

"Oh I'm sure she does my good man! I can think of at least one, rather sizeable reason, eh what!" Aldercott gestured, altogether too indelicately for a man at a ball, at his crotch. For a moment, Hemsbridge feared he might have got stuck in a time loop, back to his fourteenth birthday. But then he was distracted, very pleasingly, by a new presence in the room. For just as his so-called 'friend' was behaving like a moron, in a manner that would have been unacceptable in the Stepney docks, let alone in polite society, Lady Duckington entered the room. She was as radiant as ever, her hair worn longer than was fashionable, with a couple of curls strategically flowing over her shoulders, and wearing a delightfully elegant blue and white evening dress the like of which he had never seen before.

Immediately, his embarrassment at being in the company of Aldercott, and his boredom with the entire occasion, quite evaporated into thin air.

He was suddenly delighted to be here, at this moment, at this ball in Berkshire, with a woman such as that mere feet away from him and her acquaintance already made.

"Speak of the devil..." muttered Aldercott, bringing him back down to earth rather abruptly.

"- and what a devil too. Ravishing, I'm sure you'd agree. You won't mind holding my drink for just a moment old boy? Duty calls, eh what?"

Shoving his glass into Sterling's hand uncaringly, Aldercott set off in the direction of Lady Duckington. Damn and blast! Hemsbridge gritted his teeth and was instantly annoyed. That bounder was going to get in ahead of him! And, as far as she was concerned, there was no more between himself and Lady Duckington than the connection that existed between her and that imbecile Aldercott!

He had to act, and fast. Abandoning his own, untasted, measure of drink, as well as Aldercott's, he wove a path for himself through the assembled throng of guests, preparing his introductory words, just as Lady Duckington craned her neck to whisper something direct, and undoubtedly salacious, into Braydon Aldercott's ear...

*

Lady Olivia Asterwood had been irritated to see her son, Sterling, conversing with his boisterous old acquaintance, Aldercott, over the ornate bronze punchbowl, rather than flirting with suitable young ladies. She was positively furious to see the two of them, seemingly with one mind, converging on the person of that notorious (and worst of all, already married) hussy Lady Amelia Duckington.

Where the devil was that woman's husband, when one needed him! She needed some restraining, she was entirely too enthusiastic about leading young bachelors astray with her womanly wiles. Lady Olivia watched, lips pursed and shaking her head in horror, as the hussy and Aldercott headed off towards the terrace, Sterling trailing like a dog.

Her son appeared to have entirely forgotten his dynastic responsibility, to pursue a suitable match, in favour of some ghastly love triangle (or perhaps something even worse – she shuddered to imagine)! It was enough to make one quite abandon all decorum and succumb to a fit of the vapours.

Just at that moment though, a worthy distraction came along to take Lady Olivia's mind quite away from her son's errors. There came the noise of some tentative and well-mannered throat clearing, just behind her.

"Ahem, I hope you er, er, don't mind me interjecting in this manner…" Heavens above! It was Professor Edward Greenidge, the genealogical scholar whom she had met, only a few nights ago. Lady Hemsbridge's mood immediately lightened on seeing the learned fellow.

"My dear Professor Greenidge!" she declared warmly. "Why, it is a most pleasant surprise to see you! Has your research brought you out here to Berkshire…" and then, with a little resurgence of a much younger self, she thought to add "… or are you here for the sheer pleasure of it?"

For just a second, Lady Hemsbridge thought she saw a flicker of more than academic interest cross the reserved scholar's face.

"Alas my Lady, it is not my work that has er, er, compelled me to make an appearance at this rather charming occasion" he said, meeting her gaze anxiously, and gesturing around the room. A few couples were just starting a waltz in the centre of it, to the accompaniment of the string quartet in the corner. Normally this would have prompted a speech from Lady Hemsbridge on the risks of impropriety embodied in this new continental dance fashion, but, this time, she was too engaged with her conversation to bother.

"Rather, it is a family affair. My brother, Reginald, married the Earl of Teverson's daughter, which, rather interestingly, connected up two disparate branches of the ancient House of Poitou. Not that er, er, too many guests at the wedding were aware of the momentous historical significance behind the match, er, er..." he faltered, used to people glazing away and looking for an excuse to leave his conversations about his academic interests. However, to his pleasant surprise (and eternal gratitude), Lady Hemsbridge seemed quite taken by his insights.

"Is that so, my good sir?" she said, with genuine enthusiasm. "How fascinating. I was unaware of such a connection, far-flung as it obviously is?"

"There is a link, via a certain Sir Hugh de Lacey, who was killed in the Third Crusade, but not before he had the foresight to produce an heir. In any case, I now, er, find myself er, er, a member by marriage of a very old and distinguished Anglo-Norman lineage."

"How very fascinating professor" said Lady Hemsbridge, eyeing him with decided interest. He was getting more attractive by the day, this slightly strange man of letters.

"I suppose it is, if one has er, er, an interest in such things. Tell me my Lady…" said Greenidge, suddenly rediscovering some youthful sparkle. "- would it be improper of me to request a perambulation with you, er, around the grounds? I do find the press of people in a ballroom to be er, er, not very conducive to conversation.…"

"Why my good sir! Not improper at all! You can tell me all about the House of Poitou while we're at it…" and with that, the two older people set off, arm in arm, for a spirited conversation about family affairs.

*

Hemsbridge did not delay. Seeing that Aldercott and Lady Duckington were moving away from him, directly to the terrace, and undoubtedly into the gardens, he crossed the ballroom at a remarkably unseemly pace, heading for the double doors through which they had disappeared, not caring for the looks of shock and disapproval that his haste engendered. There was nobody on the terrace, but, instinctively, he felt he knew where they would be found. Rushing round the corner, he suddenly found himself face to face with the pair, just as Aldercott was about to place a kiss on Lady Duckington's neck, on an obvious trajectory towards the rounded delights of her breasts.

"Sorry, but might I interject?" he said boldly, without a hint of hesitation in his voice.

"Sorry, what?" Aldercott was astounded at the temerity of this interruption, staring hot hate into the eyes of his sometime friend and rival. "Can you not see, Hemsbridge, that we are occupied?"

"Yes, I can quite see that you are on the point of assailing the honour of a married woman. I wonder what the guests at the ball would think if they were to hear that you were compromising this lady, not to mention the destruction of a rather fine patch of roses, which you appear to be trampling, as they quite respectably carry on inside?"

"Old boy, I think this most impertinent of you!"

"My Lord Hemsbridge is quite correct, my Lord" Lady Duckington suddenly butted in, to the immense surprise of both men. In that moment, Hemsbridge knew that his boldness had paid off. He exchanged a glance with the Lady, who looked to him past Aldercott's stare of abject horror, smiling wryly to confirm that she was with him.

"I'm not sure what came over me, my Lord, but I presume it must have been some sort of attack of the vapours. I am quite overcome. Lord Hemsbridge I feel, would be the most suitable candidate for my resuscitation."

"I don't understand!" exclaimed Aldercott, glancing between the two parties frantically. "Is this some sort of joke? Are you two in conspiracy to humiliate me?!"

"Nothing of the sort" said Hemsbridge, physically placing himself between the two. "You, on the other hand, my good Aldercott were in conspiracy to commit adultery, and have been thwarted. I suggest you make your way back into the house to avoid a scandal. Off you trot." He waved condescendingly at his old friend (and resented blowhard), leaving Aldercott to head back inside with his tail between his legs.

He and Lady Duckington stood considering each other, now in a position to resume their affair from the previous evening, should they so choose.

For half a second Hemsbridge didn't quite know what to do. He was unsure of himself and the situation, having never been in a position such as this before (not having been in the habit of cuckolding anyone….). Here he was, standing before a married woman, with whom he had already made love and who had just, more or less, consented to him doing it again, by dismissing Aldercott and insisting that he stick around, and yet it did not seem quite clear how he ought to proceed.

Should he reach for her at once, and allow his intense and passionate style of love-making to take hold, given her enthusiasm the other night, or would that be considered impertinent, uncalled for, excessive? Should he simply talk to her a little, wait for the conversation to take a flirtatious turn, and then kiss her? Both appealed, but also had their problems. Like so many intelligent and attractive young men, he could be thoroughly indecisive in these matters – ladies were, after all, dangerously unpredictable.

Lady Duckington however, was not quite so prone to dithering.

She knew exactly what she wanted and how best to go about getting it, and so took matters (as women so often must, when confronted with the fleeting idiocy of men) into her own hands, quite literally as it happened. Taking his hands in hers, trying to ignore the diamond ring that sat upon her fourth finger, she brought his hands to where she wanted them, and sighed with pleasure as he ran his hands over some of her most sensitive areas.

"Fear not my lord" she whispered in his ear, letting her tongue lick delicately at the side of his face, serpentine and deadly. "-you have my express permission: ravish me!"

Her affirmative whisper was all the encouragement that Hemsbridge required. He pressed himself forcefully against her, quite suddenly, pushing her hard against the back wall of the artfully constructed grotto in which they hid, caring not for the fate of the well-trimmed roses he had earlier presumed to defend. He kissed her with a precise and hungry aggression, nibbling at her neck, her ears, her chin, as well as her lips, eliciting sounds of sensual pleasure from his ever eager partner.

His hands gripped her, digging into her flesh, to pin her in place and declare, with authority, that, though she was a married woman with an independent mind, in this instance, at her own admission (insistence even) she was his.

His lustful nature overwhelmed him, and, with little thought, he released his falls, hitched aside her petticoats, lifted her leg to his hip, as they leant against the wall, and penetrated her hard and fast, thrusting with confident enjoyment and smacking her deliciously heart-shaped derriere as if to encourage the whole thing along. She moaned her enjoyment against his lips, arching her body into every thrust, her need, again, as great as his.

Sterling came to an abrupt realisation, even as he drove them both towards the completion the desired. He more than liked this mode of love-making, this freedom to express the intensity of passion without fear of offending. He liked Lady Duckington's willingness to submit, her keenness to draw out his fiercest and most masculine nature.

He liked the rough physicality of it, it expressed feelings and passions he had long held, and gave relief to frustrations he had never before entirely realised he had.

He liked dominating, being in power, and crucially, to judge from her ecstatic reaction, Lady Duckington liked it rather a lot too...

*

After an earth-shattering climax that seemed to bring the very sky crashing down about them, in a blur of disorienting pleasure, they moved and made the effort to restore their hair and clothes to the level of neatness expected of members of the gentry at a ball, then slipped back inside. They had not discussed it, but, by some shared instinct for self-preservation they parted ways immediately, heading to opposite ends of the room to avoid any suspicions of association.

Despite this however, they could not seem to stop looking at each other, checking all around for the other's location all the time. Hemsbridge found himself trapped in a boring conversation about French literature with some timid debutante his mother had insisted he meet, but, despite the risk of appearing rude, he could not stop glancing over her shoulder to try and keep some track of Lady Duckington's movements.

She, for her part, did likewise. Finding herself cornered by a fat Earl, Sir Jolyon Backwagg, fourth Earl of Cheltenham, a distant acquaintance of her husband's, it was impossible to resist constant glances to the other side of the room, to the handsome face and darkly seductive presence of Sterling Asterwood, Marquess of Hemsbridge.

He had been on her mind all day, and had physically imposed himself upon her with such delicious forcefulness, it was all she could do to resist the urge to run over and kiss him again, regardless of the consequences.

"Of course, Lord Duckington was a very keen enthusiast of the steak and mustard sandwich" said Backwagg in a low, monotonous voice which could have put an insomniac springer spaniel to sleep. Lady Duckington kept smiling, nodding and then looking away, to watch her scandalous lover, chatting to some inconsequential blonde on the other side of the room.

"Everyone presumes that oaf down in Kent established it as a culinary institution, but I know better. It was your father-in law, Edmund, who was really the first to call for his beef to be delivered betwixt two sides of bread."

"Is that so, my Lord?" she said, feigning interest. "That really is rather fascinating."

"It is quite, isn't it?" said the fat old Earl, so confident of his importance that he was unable to spot sarcasm, even when it was almost slapping him firmly in the face. He was a ruddy man all over, with ginger hair and a face that indicated he had drunk too much strong claret over the years. His gut spilled forward, barely held back by a red evening coat and mustard yellow waist coat. This was the sort of company that Amelia was forced to keep, in her role as a dutiful wife of the aristocracy.

"A most satisfying hors d'oeuvres after a hard night's dancing on occasions such as this, a good beef sandwich, wouldn't you agree?"

"Quite, my Lord" said Lady Duckington, pleased to notice that Sterling was moving away from his conversation with the rather plain debutante. Her heart quickened its pace very slightly when she realised that he was moving towards her.

"Excellent to see that we are in agreement on these important matters" Backwagg spoke again, slurring a little, before taking another hearty swig of wine. "Were I a younger and, dare I say it, more athletically endowed young fellow, I might be inclined to ask you to dance myself, my Lady. As it happens, I fear I am too old, and gout-ridden to be dancing."

"Oh, my Lord is too modest," cut in Hemsbridge, suddenly emerging from the press of bodies. Lady Duckington's entire person contracted with relief. He was here! Thank God!

"Though, as you have been so decent as to decline the pleasure, might I?" he extended his hand to Lady Duckington, and, after an obliging, sozzled nod from the Earl of Cheltenham, and a barely contained grin from Lady Duckington, the pair set off for the dance floor.

Chapter Nine

To give him his due, Aldercott was the sort of man who knew when he was beaten. Having never really wanted anything from Lady Duckington except occasional access to her body, he was gracious enough to concede that what had come to pass between her and Hemsbridge was, if not yet a copper-bottomed love affair (she was after all, a married woman) then at the very least more than a passing fling. He might have been a fool in some respects, but that did not make him entirely stupid, and he knew when he was beaten, as much as he was capable of telling when the glances and touches that a couple share are more than just niceties.

Something was passing between Hemsbridge and Lady Duckington, and, though he was the first, he was certainly not the only member of high society to take note.

They were sighted together, scandalously often.

They went to the theatre, and took in a production of *Anthony and Cleopatra* at the Adelphi, the season's most fashionable theatre event. Some gossips and hacks remarked, in the society pages, that it was perhaps fitting that a pair as unorthodox as them should be sighted together, watching a tale of two well-heeled people destroyed by passion, but neither took any notice. Lady Duckington was used to idle, even vicious, gossip, it followed her wherever she went, and Hemsbridge was tough enough to cope.

They were more commonly seen together at balls, of course. They could barely be bothered to hide their affection, and soon what was passing between them was so widely reputed it barely mattered. The unwed girls stopped looking at Hemsbridge with playful longing and instead focussed their attention on other, truer bachelors.

They knew that, though unwed, he was effectively taken, no matter what their hopeful matchmaking mothers said. They could see it, in the way the two of them danced together, laughed at one another's jokes and gazed into one another's eyes for just a little longer than would be expected.

It should have been a scandal, but really Lady Duckington's extra-marital arrangements were so well known, most soon got somewhat bored with the entire affair.

Sterling's mother was unimpressed in the extreme, but he managed to still dance with enough of the insipid young ladies she wished him to pay court to, that she managed to grit her teeth and simply glare at him. He was deeply grateful for her forbearance – indeed, he wondered what might have happened, to make her respond in such a fashion.

One person who was not at all willing to ignore the affair was Lady Henrietta Latchford, a dark and slender young woman, pretty enough, now married to the Marquess of Vennington, but still attached, in an impotent way, to Hemsbridge. They had shared a brief, unconsummated summer passion, before a combination of family intervention and Hemsbridge's boredom had torn them apart.

Lady Hemsbridge had never approved of her, disdainful of the fact that her grandfather had made his fortune by setting up a string of iron mines in North Yorkshire. "Well…" she had commented "- if you want to spend your life with a girl who smells like a blast furnace, then be my guest!" It hadn't been meant to be.

"I see that you've moved on, Sterling," Lady Vennington said, at the first opportunity to pass Hemsbridge a quite word.

"I can't quite perceive what it is that you are alluding to, my lady" he replied, with a playful innocence that they both knew at once to be false. "I have passed from champagne to port, is that what you base your astute observation on?"

"Oh don't be such a bore! You know exactly what I mean! That Duckington woman, you can't take your eyes off her! Or your hands, for that matter!" Her tone was filled with scornful disapproval.

"Lady Duckington and I share a close bond of companionship - that is all…" he had said, before terminating the conversation by moving swiftly towards some other acquaintance. Lady Vennington had stared cold daggers at him, but said no more.

Nothing ruins a high-society ball more fully, or more swiftly, than accusations of scandal, even when all present know them to be true. The polite thing to do is to ignore them in public, and gossip about such things in private.

Another individual who was not so delighted to see this new coupling was Lord Waterford, a handsome but rather dim young fellow who had bedded Lady Duckington on various occasions, over quite some time.

He took it upon himself to approach first Sterling, and then Amelia, one evening, though what he was possibly hoping to achieve no-one could say:

"My Lord Hemsbridge" he had said, in the clipped manner many charmless men of the English upper class have.

"My Lord Waterford" Hemsbridge acknowledged, in his rather silkier tones.

"I see that you and Lady Duckington have become rather, fond of one another, shall we say?"

"Whatever can you mean?"

"You just watch yourself Hemsbridge" Waterford had hissed, lunging forward, trying to be menacing. Hemsbridge held his ground. "She's a married woman you know," he said it like a threat, as if he might as well have said "why shouldn't I punch you in the face?"

Hemsbridge noticed that his fists were clenched and his teeth gritted. The bluster which the anger had brought out in him had ruffled his sandy blonde hair and made his finely chiselled cheeks turn red.

"My dear Lord Waterford, you are quite obviously overwrought. I feel that, perhaps, you should have another glass of something" Hemsbridge had replied, beaming pleasantly, before leaning close to add "- that never bloody well stopped you, did it, eh Waterford?" Waterford had said nothing, glared, then walked away. He was too cowardly to declare a duel for this slight on his honour (which everyone would have known to be accurate anyway), and too stupid to think of a decent retort. He and Hemsbridge did not converse further that evening.

*

Sharing a bedchamber later on, both Hemsbridge and Lady Duckington could not help but notice that the other seemed to be holding back, as if distracted.

They made love with great energy and enthusiasm, as ever, their bodies flowing together naturally, and the pleasures they shared as intense as ever. But each could not shake the sense that the other was holding back somehow, not abandoning themselves fully to this act.

Though the motions were much the same, they lacked a certain spark. It was Lady Duckington who was the first to raise it, as she sat, hot and tingling all over, after their shared passion.

"Lord Waterford spoke to me tonight" she said, still slightly short of breath from their exertions, but in a serious tone of voice that moved the two of them beyond what they had just shared beneath the sheets.

"Oh yes?" said Hemsbridge. "He spoke to me too, briefly."

"He said that he disapproved of us, of this, I should say, and that many others did as well."

"Well, he would say that wouldn't he?"

"He said that it was morally wrong, and we'd be disgraced, and not just ourselves, but our whole families, if it ever got out."

"Thwarted passion can make people say silly things from time to time. I doubt anything will come of it" Hemsbridge said with feigned confidence. He nevertheless rose up in bed, roused by a swelling concern.

"Doubtless he has some, not entirely difficult to grasp, feelings of envy towards me, you, towards..." he paused for a second, mulling the word he was about to use, suppressing the instinct but then going with it anyway, "- towards us."

"Oh Sterling" said Lady Duckington, planting a small kiss on his arched shoulder blade. "I hope to God you're right" their bodies came together, and they resumed their enjoyment of passion.

Chapter Ten

To both complicate and simplify matters in equal measure, Lady Duckington soon learned that her husband was, in fact, truly unwell. She received a note from him, written in the firm hand of his valet, Macclesfield, but nevertheless still indicating the frailty of old age in full. As he was dictating, Lord Duckington had obviously mixed and slurred his words, and his meaning at times was not entirely clear. The thrust of it was that he had been staying on the Sussex coast not to only catch up with old friends, but also on the serious counsel of his physician, who was of the belief that fresh air and regular light exercise might be the old peer's last remaining hope of prolonging his life. Out of a mixture of kindness and fear, he had not informed his wife, instead claiming that his sojourn was a purely social affair. Now however, he had grasped the real truth and was forced to confess it, he was dying, and he wanted his good wife at his side.

Moved by a combination of human sympathy, marital piety, and concern for her inheritance, Lady Duckington immediately arranged a carriage to convey her due south, out of London to the seaside.

*

The sight of Lord Duckington immediately confirmed all of her hopes and fears at once. He was deeply unwell.

The corpulence he had acquired in old age had partly been stripped away, he had lost a worrying amount of weight, and the usual ruddy cheer that was in his cheeks had faded, replaced by a grey, gaunt look and haggard features that did not flatter him.

His breathing was heavy and irregular, and his grey hair appeared to have grown thin. Almost all of the youthful glimmer of energy and faded charm, which he had retained even into his '70s, and which Amelia had grown rather fond of over time, (her frequent infidelities notwithstanding) had now left him.

Instead, he had the look of sadness and resignation that comes over one who knows that they are very soon to die.

"My darling wife..." his voice was frail and shaky as she entered his bedchamber.

He went to hold out his hand, but the doctor quickly took it, and gently returned it to the bed to prevent any unnecessary exertion of energy.

For the moribund, even the most basic of courtesies become impossible, as mind, body and soul drift away from the world and into whatever ether awaits us.

"Percival" she said, foregoing formality.

"It warms my heart to see you, I only wish under more auspicious circumstances."

"Please, Amelia," he spoke weakly.

"It is quite all right. I am a very old man, and have lived well, in my way. We both of us knew that it would reach this terminus, when we set out on our journey together."

He mustered what she could interpret as a smile.

Though his mouth struggled to crack into the expression, his eyes, still grey-blue and distinctive, managed a little twinkle of life, of real joy. It was a heart-warming glimpse of his soul, and she appreciated it.

"I believe that Runciman has some business to discuss. Please, do not let common sentimentality deter you from it, I won't have you sitting around feeling sorry for yourself on my account."

Leaning back into his pillows, Lord Duckington made a slight gesture, indicating that his solicitor, Mr. Harold Runciman, who was standing by a cabinet, in the upright, austere manner he always had, should now step forward and speak:

"Lady Duckington, it is good of you to have made the journey down from the capital. As my Lord indicates, there are a few delicate matters of a legal nature to discuss, owing to his..." he pondered his next word. It doesn't do to remind the dying of their situation, but it could not be helped, "-condition."

He finally made his mind up, nodding discreetly to the old Lord, who seemed already to be half asleep.

"As you are no doubt aware," Runciman continued "Lord Duckington has no legitimate or indeed, illegitimate, issue. With no sons or daughters to succeed him, his estate and titles are due to pass to another relative, his second cousin twice removed, a Mr. Alfred Percival Redmayne, who I believe is a resident of the Scottish Highlands, as it happens. Nevertheless, my Lord has made considerable provision in his will for your upkeep after he passes. So you need not be concerned for yourself - a considerable portion of the monetary fortune, as well as certain other moveable and immoveable assets have been designated as your inheritance."

"That is comforting indeed to know" replied Lady Duckington, concealing her small disappointment at not inheriting the entirety of the unentailed fortune and properties, behind a veneer of politeness that befitted the situation.

"Thank you very much, Runciman" Lord Duckington panted, coughing slightly and getting up in bed in a manner which clearly alarmed the doctor.

"Now that that trifle is out of the way, my darling Amelia, it falls to me to say this. I know, and have known since we were betrothed, that I am not, and never was, the husband of a young girl's dreams. I know that my age, and certain other characteristics which one might attribute to me, do not make me the most attractive match in the stakes that truly matter, certainly to the young and vigorous. Nevertheless, I hope that, in my modest way, I have provided you with some happiness, and what might be termed a good life, for you have brought an old man untold joy in his dying years." He paused a moment, catching his breath.

"You have my blessing, do not mourn for me any more than is expected of you by society, go into the world, and find happiness renewed."

"Thank you my Lord!" Amelia said, rushing over to him and kissing his wrinkled hands, overcome by a spontaneous affection. It was the most honest and openly loving he had ever been towards her, and her appreciation was true and heartfelt. He was a curmudgeonly old man, it was true, and she had never found him attractive, but he was kind, and he had been generous of spirit towards her in their years together, for surely he had known of her indiscretions, yet he had never once berated her for them.

"Oh thank you! Your words are truly generous! I shall honour them, fear not, your wishes shall be honoured."

"I know they will, Amelia" he said, with another flickering smile. "I know they will."

Chapter Eleven

"I'd attribute it to that injection of peasant fecundity" chuckled Lady Garret, between mouthfuls of tea and scones. Just days after visiting her dying husband, Lady Duckington was back in London for the continuation of the social season. She was in two minds. It seemed inappropriate to be here, ostensibly enjoying herself with her husband on a provincial death bed, yet it had also been his wish, and she had an obligation to him, and to herself, to carry on with her life. Admittedly though, sitting around gossiping with a gaggle of sycophantic hens hadn't quite been what she had in mind.

"Stanningfield is virile enough of course, as I imagine many of us were all too aware" Lady Garret continued, nodding not-all-that subtly in the direction of her host. It was fairly common knowledge that Lady Duckington had had a brief fling with the handsome Suffolk Earl, before he had turned eccentric and run off with a poor schoolmistress.

"My mother always maintained, and I believe this was the opinion of her physician as well, that a little of the blood of the labouring classes can actually help the nobility in breeding. Well, of course, they multiply like rabbits in those farmhands out in East Anglia - it's neither proper nor Christian!"

"Perhaps that is why she married him!" said another guest, the buck-toothed Lady Orpington, who had a long history of resenting those more attractive, and seasoned in the arts of love-making, than herself. She drew a few hooting laughs from the assembled ladies, then went back to her tea.

"Indeed!" Lady Garret continued. "She had an impeccable lineage, but that didn't keep the lowly manners of her upbringing at bay! Shame really, to inherit a peasant's virility but a church mouse's timidity. Silly little girl must have been absolutely desperate, Christ only knows what Stanningfield saw in her."

They had recently learned that Catherine Rockingham nee Thornberry, Stanningfield's unexpected bride, was with child, and due to bear him an heir. It would be the first heir of the de Quincy line to be born into a noble household for over a century, though goodwill at this resurrection of a prime mediaeval bloodline was somewhat lacking, at least in certain quarters of the gentry...

All this talk of pregnancy, however, was not what Lady Duckington wanted. It was all far too painful and difficult to take, bringing up thoughts and memories of an anguish she thought she had long ago buried. Mocking the pregnant was one thing, but in so doing, her assembled acquaintances were also mocking her, by proxy, for her lack of pregnancy.

Lord Duckington had provided much, but no child, and now she was forced to face the mounting fear that no-one ever would. She had been tempted, whilst enjoying her young lovers, to allow the possibility of pregnancy, but the truth would have become known, and she could not find it in herself to pass off another man's child as her husband's. So she had been careful, and mostly, made sure that her lovers took measures to avoid the chance of a child. But the lack nagged at her - she was getting older, and her amorous future was uncertain, Sterling Asterwood notwithstanding.

Over the past few days, thoughts of the Marquess of Hemsbridge had brought her nothing but angst. Her attraction to him was growing, that much was clear. Despite her heart having been locked in a loveless marital cage for years, she knew its ways and its desires, enough to have the sense that she wanted him, that her feelings could grow to something more. The crucial question, which rapidly became plain, but to which the answer was complex, was - did he want her? He certainly lusted after her - indeed, he was all too willing to run his firm Somerset hands over her body, in a manner that was forceful but utterly exciting to her. He had introduced her to new physical sensations, new dynamics that she had not previously encountered, either in her uninspiring marital bed, or in her fleeting liaisons with society dandies.

It was all too much, for any soon-to-be widow, approaching the upper limits of her natural fecundity, to bear. Though it was painful to admit, and all too awkward, she needed a man who might marry her, and not be put off by her much gossiped about past, if she was ever to have a child of her own.

Hemsbridge was, so far, the only even faintly possible candidate for that role, but, as yet, she had no sign from him, no indication of his intent in his association with her, nor any clarity as to his true feelings.

Until Percival passed, and she was in a position for any man to consider her for marriage, she could not even truly consider what might happen. She knew that there was a real risk that the children, whom she had felt, since she was a girl, it was her destiny to bring into the world, would remain nothing more than shimmers in her eye, dimming every year, as she grew older, and the gentlemen slowly started to lose interest.

She refused to contemplate the possibility that those children might not happen, it hurt too much to think of it. So she threw herself at the world. She did as any cornered and wounded animal does, when its tormentors have the gall to stand directly over it: she lashed out.

"Well of course, perhaps all of us assembled could use a small injection of Miss Thornberry's peasant fecundity, as you so eloquently put it my dear Lady Garret" she exclaimed sharply, drawing looks of surprise from all, for it was the first time she had spoken in a while.

"You, for example, Lady Orpington. Perhaps you would benefit from a little lower class promiscuity. After all, such gifts might at last tempt Lord Orpington away from his preferred hobby of buggering serving boys in the back rooms of your house, and back into your skinny, bony bosom. If only for some healthy country genes, you might have a set of front teeth a decent gentleman could bear to look at."

"My lady! I must protest in the strongest possible terms…" but Lady Duckington cut her off. She was in a brutal mood, sadistic even, and determined to take it out on her resented guests with her acid tongue. The habits of a lifetime, of defending herself from the mean spirited by attacking them first, took over, and her turbulent emotions drove her to be nastier than ever.

"And you, Lady Garret, you too would probably benefit from some labourers' inheritance. After all, the healthy glow and open manner of the honest country bumpkin might actually have landed you a husband, rather than an elaborate set of imitation bone china, and some cats."

"Lady Duckington! You insult your own good name with this absurd outburst…" but once more, the protesting guest was cut off, by the swift turn of the head of her vicious hostess.

"And as for you, my good Lady Wilmington" she hissed, directing her serpentine attention and sharp tongue at her third acquaintance present.

"Maybe some hard toil in the fields is what is required in your case. Working off all those fondant fancies you stuff into your over-wide gullet might reduce some of the excess fat which keeps Captain Wilmington at sea, doing God knows what heinous acts, to God knows what pox-ridden foreign whores, rather than returning to your creaking marriage bed and the flatulent wife he must share it with."

"Never have I been so insulted in my entire life!" said Lady Wilmington, rising to her feet and red with anger.

"You bring shame to your name and house, Lady Duckington, and I, for one, am not going to sit here and be insulted. Good day to you!" she slammed down her tea cup and stormed out, with Ladies Garret and Orpington following at once. They harrumphed their way out of the front door and to their carriages, leaving Lady Duckington to sit and brood.

*

Amelia barely mustered the energy to go out to a ball that night. She had known it was in her social calendar, indeed, the invitation had sat, heavy and almost threatening, above her mantelpiece for weeks, with so many others during the busy social Season. Part of her did not wish to go, after all, her husband was dying and she was facing one of the greatest personal crises of her life. But she considered that it would have been churlish not to attend, would, indeed, have simply given the *ton* yet more chance to gossip about her, and so she found some reserve of vitality, and pushed herself (if that were indeed possible) out the door.

She realised, as soon as she arrived, that the principal attraction, although she had been hiding her motivations from herself, had been the thought that Sterling might be there. It seemed eminently possible, for they would have struggled to avoid each other's company, accidental or otherwise, over the past weeks. And, truth to tell, she had been glad, every time, when circumstance threw them together, no matter what propriety might indicate.

Almost inevitably, however, he was not in attendance. Perhaps the demands of society were taking it out of him. Perhaps he was sick of dancing and conversing with bores.

Perhaps his mother had got wind of the affair, locked him in a cellar and thrown away the key. Whatever the reason, he was not there, and this forced Lady Duckington to confront the inconvenient reality that she knew lay before her - that her feelings for this handsome young Marquess were running away from her, and, unlike with her previous casual affairs, this was fast becoming a real romantic attachment.

'Oh if only Sterling were here!' she found herself thinking, sighing, her facial muscles tired from forcing herself to smile at so many tedious suitors. Her past was coming back to haunt her, with all of these self-serving men, looking simply for their own physical gratification, expecting her to instantly agree to go off into the secluded corners of the gardens with them. Where before they had seemed somewhat charming, now they seemed shallow and uncaring.

Sterling was a better-looking man than any of these pompous oafs, and at least twice the value of any of them as a conversationalist. She longed for him, yearned for him to be at her side, his absence was gnawing at her, and, despite her wish to deny the intensity of her own feelings, would continue to do so until he re-emerged into her life, and made his feelings, whatever they may be, as clear as the cut crystal glass she was now holding in her hand.

A little earlier in the day, not so very far away, although some distance from London and high society, Hemsbridge's mind was occupied. It was not so occupied that no thought at all of Lady Duckington had managed to force its way in, but alas, such pleasant notions had to be pushed aside for now. For now, in his capacity as Marquess of Hemsbridge, lord and master of an extensive West Country estate, Hemsbridge was busy with a few matters of business.

"Yes Mr. Smithers, I can quite see that!" he said, examining a ledger. His man of business, a Mr. Arkwright Smithers of Taunton, was standing at his shoulder, dressed in his usual plain black garb and bringing some troubling accounts to his attention.

"- but where the devil have these blasted funds gone!"

"Well…" said the man of business, with a weary look. He was used to explaining such concerns to the nobility, who generally found them tiresome. A man like Hemsbridge would always rather be with his horses or his mistresses than poring over ledgers and crunching numbers in the presence of clerks. Smithers was experienced enough to know this, and aimed always to be brief.

"… it appears that there are only two possible explanations. The first is that there could have been some error in our book-keeping, which would be, I hasten to add, something of a first at a reputable firm like Smithers and Sons. I can assure you my Lord, our records have been checked and triple-checked, and there is no such omission to be found."

"Yes, yes Smithers" said Hemsbridge, impatient. "I'm sure you've done terribly good work, as you have for generations for my family. But all these pleasantries aside, what the deuce has become of these funds!"

"That leads us neatly on to the second possibility" said Smithers, looking quietly pleased with himself. Numbers, and the explanation of numbers, was his field, his speciality. His expertise gave him a brief taste of superiority over his better-bred employer, and he relished it.

"We have received reports that one of your estate managers, a Mr. MacGregor, I believe, of Scots extraction, has been behaving in a rather unorthodox fashion, unbecoming of an esteemed employee of a house as ancient as yours, my Lord. He has been known to give tenants of yours an undue degree of, shall we say, 'drama' in his monthly rent collections, often arriving drunk, and behaving in a violent and churlish manner alongside the gangs of ruffians he employs."

Smithers looked slightly ill at the thought of such behaviour.

"As the accountancy indiscretion can be traced to the estate that he manages, I think it fair to assume that, as well as behaving in a manner unbefitting a professional servant of a great estate, he may also have, as one's cruder tavern companions might have it, 'greased his own palms', my Lord."

"This expression is unfamiliar to me Smithers" said Hemsbridge, comprehending enough to know that all this spelt trouble. "Please explain."

"MacGregor has been embezzling funds. He has taken rent at above the figure at which you, according to my counsel, have set it, and moreover, he has not handed over all of the monies he was owing to you, pending their collection. What he has chosen to do with said monies is between himself, and his God, though the act of having done so is now between you, he, and Blind Lady Justice herself. My recommendation would be that your Lordship move to discipline the unruly fellow post-haste. Indeed, this does seem a matter in which to involve the magistrate."

"A sound plan Smithers, as ever" Hemsbridge replied, struggling to contain his shock. MacGregor! Embezzling funds and roughing up tenants! This was beyond unacceptable. Hemsbridge had always considered himself a fair master and a reasonable man of upstanding morals, and to have an employee of his prowling the countryside and intimidating poor farmers, for the purposes of lining his own pockets, was repulsive to him. And after all, what if anyone in society found out! It would bring terrible shame to the good name of Hemsbridge.

There was nothing the aristocracy looked down on more, than tyrannical management of one's estates. A gentleman should be firm but fair in his exercise of power, and certainly not abuse it for personal gain. He had a responsibility to his family, to his honour, and to his unfortunate tenants, to sort this out immediately.

"Thank you Smithers" he said, throwing on his coat and making for the door. "That will be all. I will see to this immediately." And he stormed out, wishing that he might administer old-fashioned feudal justice, rather than needing to wait for the magistrate.

*

All of the unpleasantness of the MacGregor affair left a bitter taste in Hemsbridge's mouth. Moreover, it left him weary and overwrought, and made Lady Amelia Duckington seem all the more distant from his tedious day to day reality, of book-keeping and maternal taps on the wrist. He was to receive another later that evening, as he and Lady Hemsbridge, despite his protestations that he was tired and had business to attend to the next day, attended another ball, this time hosted by Lord Staines, in Berkshire.

His lack of enthusiasm showed. He could tell immediately. Guests turned politely to greet him, then shrunk away with an odd mixture of disapproval and discomfort at the sight of his slightly wild eyes and generally unpleasant demeanour. Once he had escaped his mother's attention, as she was busy gossiping with a bishop, whom she had known as a child, he skulked around the edges of the room, eyeing young ladies not so much out of lust as from a sense of frustration at the utter undesirability of any of them, for the role of wife.

A distant acquaintance, Goddard, offered him a drink, but soon recoiled in the face of his surly lack of conversation, muttering that they would catch up later and presuming that some tragedy had befallen the Hemsbridge family.

Hemsbridge almost forgot about Amelia until he saw her. It had been often like this with young ladies, that they used a gentleman's envy of others, and fear of loss of the lady's attentions, as a force to propel a man's feelings forward. He disliked, intensely, being manipulated in such a way, but had to admit that he had, all too often, been caught in exactly that trap. He had dimly hoped it would be different with Lady Duckington, but seeing her at the centre of a circle of men, the only woman in the group, wearing a striking red gown and flirting like a French sailor's wife, filled him with longing and a new, more focussed mode of anger, one he willingly turned back at the world, with force.

Rather than prowling, unsettled and irritable, as he had since arriving at the ball, he now pounced, like an experienced hunter bringing down its prey, outpacing and out-powering rivals in pursuit of the prize. He firmly, and rather impolitely, elbowed his way past the Viscount Tewkesbury, almost shoved the Marquess of Hythe aside, and cut off Lord Jeffrey St. John of Peterborough in mid-sentence.

"Lady Duckington, I believe that we have an urgent appointment on the terrace" he almost hissed, firmly placing her hand on his arm and moving her, rather forcibly, towards the doors. Momentarily turning back towards the stunned silence and ruffled cravats he had left behind him, he said merely: "- you will excuse us, gentlemen" and pushed through the doors into the open air.

Lady Duckington was, characteristically, not slow to respond to this strange interruption, nor did she seek to repress her evident feeling of distress and ire.

"What the devil do you think you're playing at Sterling!?" she snapped at him, struggling very hard not to raise her voice and alarm the other guests. "Am I not permitted, now, to enjoy the companionship of other gentlemen?"

"Oh really, Amelia!" he replied, laughing, a little harshly. "That lot of old bores? I should fancy I saved you from a bout of insomnia, nattering away to those idiots back there!"

"On what basis do you presume to know the content of their conversation, hmm?" she replied, her anger aroused by her own feelings about the situation – which was, indeed, exactly as he said, plus a great happiness that he had arrived. It was a happiness which she felt herself silly to indulge in. "On the basis of some mystical power, bestowed on you by a gypsy? Or perhaps on the basis of that most unflattering of traits in a man: jealousy!"

"Jealousy! How dare you!" he pressed his face close to hers, raising his voice in a moment of self-righteous anger. She had pricked the outer shell of his honour, and indignation oozed out.

"What do you mean how dare you? That's what it is, isn't it?" he stared at her, glowered at her, furled his brow and snarled, for, loath as he was to admit it, he suspected that she was correct.

She watched him, eyebrow raised.

The idea of this dominance was exciting to her. The practise of it was too, behind closed doors, consensually, when they were wrapped in each other's arms. But here, with him exerting himself in this way, making physical what, until then had only been an emotional power, she did not like it quite so much. What on earth had come over the two of them? She did not know, and in that moment, she was too overwhelmed to think or ask such questions.

"This is absurd!" he said, breaking away, lessening the sense of threat. "You're a married woman, and we are, at least in the eyes of the gossip mongers, if not in a way that can be publicly seen, an acknowledged pair, I suppose you could say. I shouldn't feel like I have to do this, but you just can't help yourself can you?!"

"You don't have to do anything Sterling, in fact, you have no right to!" She spoke firmly, the hard edge of anger in her tone barely constrained. "I can do as I damn well please at social events. You have no claim over me. It's just your stupid masculine pride talking. Now if you'll excuse me, I have a soiree to enjoy." She bustled away from him without any further explanation, leaving him to his own tumultuous thoughts.

She regretted that her conversation with Sterling had come to such a point. She had spoken her feelings and held her ground, and that, at least, was better than feeling uncertain. He had been playing on her mind, filling her thoughts all day, but for him to come crashing into her conversation like that, with such arrogance, such possessive pomposity was too much. No matter how bored she was with the shallow men surrounding her, his behaviour had been completely unacceptable.

Amelia thought now, away from him, that it was partly the shock of the disappointment in his behaviour, after she had spent the early part of the evening, like a green girl, longing for his presence, which had brought this out in her. All of her accumulated hope for something different, transmuted, had spilled out in a single outburst. Mentally, she castigated herself as a fool, for having hoped at all, and slipped back through the ballroom, avoiding all conversation.

Excusing herself with an imaginary megrim, she left the ball at once, after the briefest of words with the hosts.

*

Sterling was also deflated. A footman came up to him, offering him some sweet, fashionable liqueur or other but he waved him away, demanding brandy.

He needed something stiff and intense, after that shouting match in the garden *'What the devil is wrong with that woman?!'* he kept repeating to himself, over and over again, under his breath, as he stared hot contempt at the room in general.

Even as he fumed about her attitude, part of him watched the room, wondering where she had gone, wanting to see her.

Standing in a corner, with a brooding look, seemed to make him look dark, dangerous and interesting, inconveniently. Several young ladies tried to attract his attention, in the hopes of initiating conversation, presuming, in their immature and clumsy way, that they could be his saviour, the soft and sweet force that would bring him out of his fever of rage.

One such pretty young thing was the host's daughter, Lady Eliza, who, taking advantage of her role as a member of the hosts family, was brave enough to approach him, fluttering her eyelashes and fidgeting with her long, strawberry blonde hair.

"Is something to your dissatisfaction, my Lord?" she stuttered at him, shyly, unused to approaching gentlemen in this way, but feeling compelled to do so, this time, by the aura of dark intrigue that clung to the Marquess of Hemsbridge this evening.

"Alas, no" he replied perversely. "Were my mood quite so simple an affair, I would take it upon myself to raise it with your butler, or perhaps my host, your father. But this night holds greater complexity for me. You will excuse me my Lady."

Barely bothering to make eye contact, he delivered a sketchy bow and pushed away from her through the throng into the corridor.

He considered his options.

They were barely an hour's drive outside London, and the night was still young. He could get into a carriage (without his mother of course) and enjoy a night of carousing, gambling and drinking with some acquaintances or other, who would no doubt be willing to put him up for the night.

But then, no, he thought, the effort seemed too great.

There was a weariness he could sense, creeping up on him, no doubt a product of his day of business, and the unfortunate argument he had just conducted with Lady Duckington.

On reflection, such a trip was not an appealing prospect, and so, instead, Hemsbridge headed home, to his mother's disgust, bracing himself throughout for the confrontation he must surely pursue tomorrow with his embezzling estate manager.

Chapter Thirteen

Hemsbridge rose early and met Smithers in a tavern by the Taunton road. The two men, tired, sombre, ready for a difficult day's work, merely nodded at one another, and got into Hemsbridge's carriage. There was a contrast between the two of them, the middle class professional in his austere black suit, his collar and cravat neat and simple, his hair tightly cropped, and Hemsbridge, who seemed quite the dandy beside him.

The London fashion for a certain elegant flamboyance, with slim-fitting boots, breeches, and coats, combined with vivacious colours and extravagant collars and cuffs, all seemed rather alien to Mr. Smithers of Taunton. He kept his disapproval quiet though, knowing where the power and the money lay in this relationship. In private, he had heard a little of what the Marquess of Hemsbridge got up to, at society balls, the sort of company he kept, both male and, most scandalously for a confirmed bachelor, female.

To an upstanding and industrious man of work like Smithers, it was all pretty horrifying, but again he said nothing. It was not his family funding this gilded carriage, these fine glossy horses, the liveried footman, or, for that matter, his professional fee. Best let the gentry have their world, and stick firmly to his.

It was the first of August. Summer was thinking of sliding towards autumn, the grass was thick and yellowing at the edges, the trees almost heavy with an abundance of leaves. There was a slight dew on the ground, soon to be burned off in a blaze of summer sunshine. As they rattled along the dirt of the road, they could see the farmers out in the fields, getting ready for the coming autumn's harvest.

They would do a long day's work, then sip their cider and sing old country songs, a scene little changed for over a thousand years. For centuries men like Hemsbridge had ridden through this country, with its rolling hills, rich pastures and fertile fields. The birds twittered in the hedgerows, and the clouds wheeled lazily over all their heads. It was all quite as it should be, thought Hemsbridge, allowing a small smile of satisfaction to penetrate his tired haze.

One thing that was not as it should be, however, was the situation with this MacGregor fellow. A combination of anxiety about how the day would go, and the stiff brandy he had served himself on arriving home, had given Hemsbridge a fitful night. It was beyond unacceptable for a manager in his employ to abuse his power, bully his tenants and drag his name through the Somerset mud. It would all have to be corrected, forcefully, if necessary. They would collect the magistrate in the nearby town, but, as insurance, beside him sat a hard mahogany cudgel.

He had never used it, and it was polished to a sheen. He feared having to knock a little of that polish off today.

"Do you know much about this MacGregor chap, Smithers?" Hemsbridge yawned, after more than twenty minutes of silent travel.

"I can't say I have passed more than a few moments, here and there, in his company my Lord" Smithers said, stifling his own urge to yawn out of respect. "He is a rather coarse fellow, although that characteristic can be desirable in a farming foreman, even, perhaps in an estate manager. Nevertheless, I fear we may have misjudged the extent of his, ah... lowness, somewhat, in this case."

"It sounds as if you may be right."

"Not far now, I believe." Smithers leaned out of the window, letting in a blast of densely fresh rural air. "Yes, it's just over this next ridge here." Hemsbridge was relieved – it had been a long time since he had visited this estate – far too long, obviously.

*

After a short stop in the town, where, to Hemsbridge's horror, they discovered that the Magistrate had succumbed to a nasty fever and recently died, which left him, as the local Lord, as the default Magistrate, they proceeded to MacGregor's cottage. They cottage pulled up outside was ramshackle, surrounded by weed-ridden fields and unkempt hedgerows. Stepping into a puddle of mud which besmirched his fine leather boots in an instant, Hemsbridge was appalled.

If his father could see this travesty! MacGregor's part of the estate had been entirely neglected. The man was clearly unsuitable for his post. Taking the cudgel firmly in his hand, he strode powerfully towards the unpainted front door, bracing himself for an altercation, with Smithers picking his way nervously behind. It would have been clear to any onlooker which of the two handled the numbers, and which was the man of action.

After a few stern knocks, the door swung open. It revealed a rugged looking man, tall and stout, barely dressed, his undone shirt exposing a powerful, muscular frame. He had sandy red hair and an untrimmed beard, half masking his craggy features, as rough as the Scottish Highlands from which he hailed. Peering into the sunlight, the man looked, at first, aggressive, his breath reeking of last night's alcohol. Then, perceiving the fine carriage, and the fine clothes of the man in front of him, he snapped to attention.

"Crivens!" he exclaimed, his accent broad, but comprehensible to Hemsbridge, who had spent a little time in Edinburgh in his youth.

"Bugger me Auntie Mabel sideways with a rusty ladle! You're the bloody laird, ain't ye?" Choosing to ignore the profanity, Hemsbridge responded:

"I am indeed, sir, your employer, the Marquess of Hemsbridge. I had hoped that such a visit as this would be unnecessary, when I advertised for a new estate manager, and deferred this matter of business to the good judgement of Mr. Smithers here." Smithers nodded nervously at this acknowledgement.

"Alas, it would seem I was at fault in that assumption. It seems that you have been not only harassing my tenants in a most deplorable and un-Christian manner, but also pilfering funds that are not yours to take, and, judging by the state of your cottage…" he gestured at the dilapidated state of what had once been one of the finest rural cottages in all of Somerset, but was now a tatty mess.

"… wasting it all on drink, in the local taverns. What have you to say for yourself?"

"It's nay true! None of it, my Lord!" he grovelled, with an affected innocence unfitting of a man of his considerable physical endowment. "It's all hearsay! You cannae believe everything your man of business tells ye! The tenants all love me, and the money thing's just a misunderstanding!"

"That all seems somewhat difficult to believe, given the weight of evidence against you. Mr Smithers…" Smithers stepped forward, brandishing his ledger as if it were a holy text.

"We have it here in the accounts, a considerable discrepancy, all traceable to your jurisdiction, as well as an extensive written record of your crimes, as testified to by many of my tenants, and several third party witnesses. There's no use pleading with me, Mr. MacGregor, I know what you have done. You may remain in residence here, for two weeks, to give you the opportunity to find alternative employment elsewhere, but, as of now, consider our professional relationship to be terminated. Should you go near my estate, or my tenants, from now until you leave, you will be summarily removed and imprisoned. I suggest that you accept my generosity, and remove yourself from this locality as soon as possible. Good day to you, sir."

Hemsbridge stepped away with a flourish, leaving MacGregor speechless. After a moment MacGregor began to speak, but was quelled with a look from Hemsbridge – it was obvious that his thinking had finally caught up with things, and he had decided that dismissal was far better than arrest.

For Hemsbridge, it was gratifying not to have needed to use the rough force of the cudgel. The word was always preferable to the weapon in these delicate matters. As they mounted the carriage for the return journey, he muttered to Smithers:

"Do you think I was fair, sir, in my treatment of him?"

"Fair my lord?! Why I'd say you were positively saintly! Why, were our situations reversed, I'd have gone in there and run him through with an ancestral sword!"

"Good lord Smithers!" Hemsbridge laughed. "It is perhaps best that the fates dictated that our positions be as they are! Why if every nobleman in the kingdom took your view, there'd be not a single farmhand left to tend the fields!" With a hearty laugh, shared by both of them, the carriage set off, with the Marquess of Hemsbridge content that he had preserved his family's honour. But he would be having MacGregor watched, until he was gone, to be certain that the issue was well and truly dealt with.

Lady Amelia Duckington was not best pleased. Her servants had observed this mood in her many times before and were used to it, knowing to keep their distance wherever possible, but be attentive to her needs when necessary.

This time however, it took all the subtlety and tact of their profession to judge the scenario effectively. A true darkness had come over their mistress, beyond anything that they had seen previously, and they speculated as to what could possibly have brought it on.

"I heard tell..." whispered Annie Gosford, one of the chambermaids "- that she had been with child but that it were strangled in the womb and come out stillborn, lately like."

"Stuff and nonsense!" replied the Housekeeper, Mrs. Atherton, in her Lancashire burr.

"Did you ever hear such rubbish? Did you see any sign of a pregnancy my girl, in the preceding weeks? I sincerely doubt it, for there was none. No, what's got our Lady in this great huff is the impending demise of our Lord. It is quite proper that she be mourning his passing, which I have heard is soon to come, God save him."

"True as that may be…" chipped in one of the footmen, Fletcher, a fellow more inclined to gossip than is generally considered seemly in a man. "… I fear the distress facing our lady may be a little more complex than all that. She has known, for a long while, as have we all for that matter, that the passing of our master was likely imminent, and though they have never quarrelled it is hard to imagine she has ever been over fond of the old chap."

"True enough" Mrs. Atherton agreed. "Fond of his money she may have been, but I'd speculate she's set to get hold of a fair portion of that, come his passing."

"No…" continued Fletcher "- it is my belief that it is not over her moribund husband that Lady Duckington has got into this great huff, but over something else. I'd wager…" he cast around a conspiratorial glance, clearly worried that some more senior person might overhear his chatter. "- that this is all concerning one of her lovers. There's plenty enough of 'em." At this, the other two servants nodded seriously, and returned at once to their work.

*

In truth, Fletcher was completely right.

Lady Duckington was depressed, and Sterling was the cause, the force that had pressed down upon her mood and made her feel quite ill at ease with the world, and all that was in it. For days now, she had languished in her house, at once uncertain of her feelings and knowing, but not wishing to admit to herself, exactly what they were, caught in a confused haze of pain and disappointment.

A part of her wished to blame herself.

After all, she had not needed to flirt with all of those men at the ball. She had been unable to resist the urge, even though she had known it was wrong, for she had never intended to indulge in an assignation with any of them, no matter what they might have expected. She had rapidly regretted the impulse to flirt, though, God knows, she had no idea what else to do at a ball, when they had proven how shallow, and utterly boring they all were.

Inappropriate as it was, her heart yearned for Sterling Asterwood, for the Marquess of Hemsbridge, but she was struggling to break a habit she had formed over what seemed nigh-on half a lifetime's unfulfilling marriage.

The attentions of men, sordid affairs and baseless flings, carried on in hedgerows and in shady garden grottos, were what had sustained her throughout the lean and otherwise mostly sexless years of her marriage to Lord Duckington.

Now that a man had come along, a man that she could respect, a man that excited her in ways she had never previously experienced, and an eligible bachelor at that, who might relieve her of this sadness, she did not know how to behave.

So, she carried on as before, goading women and flirting outrageously with men, with neither sincerity nor conviction, not knowing, if anything, what she hoped to achieve, but merely turning and turning, on and on, like a windmill in a stiff breeze. She was repeating a pattern that no longer served her, simply because she had not the least concept of how to do anything else.

Now, however, that turning and turning had had a consequence. It had delivered a problem for her; namely the spat she and Sterling had had at the last ball. It angered her somewhat to have to face such a blatant affront to her freedom. For she had been used to a far greater freedom than most women, with her aged husband so rarely in town, and his willingness to let her run rather wild.

Men liked to control women, and she knew this, they were easily angered and jealous creatures, who did not take what they saw as insults to their honour lying down. But despite all of that, she knew that he had had a point – they had been very much in each other's company, to both their satisfaction, and some expectation could rightly have been said to have been created. The knowledge of that truth, the guilt, was tearing her apart.

A strange sort of fear, which she did not think she had ever known before, came to her. It was a worry, an anxiety, an almost physical quivering of the heart, of the body, that was hard to explain, but impossible to dismiss. She realised that it was a fear of loss, of losing him, a fear that she might never see him again or, much worse, that they might never share tenderness and intimacy again.

A fear that maybe he had lost interest in her, or, worse, that her behaviour had so alienated him, that he could not stand to see her again. Both thoughts horrified her so much that she could hardly bear to contemplate them. What had she done, that was so wrong? If only she could see into his thoughts, she thought, see what he saw, and perceive what he perceived. But she knew that was impossible.

She considered the possibility of sending him a letter. She began many drafts, some in her head, some actually committed to paper. But, somehow, she could not find the words to ask, the words to convey her thoughts and feelings, or enquire into his - the very second that she took up the pen, a certain despair overcame her. There were quite simply no words. What on earth could she say? Even when she could muster the energy to commit something to paper, she immediately lost faith in the entire enterprise, and had to lay the pen back down, get up from the escritoire, and pace tensely, like a caged animal, trying to work out how on earth she could convey to him the depth of her feelings, and the anguish of her regret.

A small group of acquaintances arrived for a morning visit, and politeness compelled her to provide them with tea, and subject herself to polite conversation. She considered asking them for advice, but then thought better of it. They were shallow sycophants, one and all, and had no real interest in her affairs, except as gossip fodder. They had come to ogle her expensive furnishings and lovely bone china, to be waited on by her liveried servants, and to spread idle gossip about like muck on new-ploughed fields. She shuddered as she considered how like them she had been, for so long.

She even, momentarily, considered asking her servants for advice. They must have some idea, she thought, of the travails of the heart. Surely they would have witnessed some of the blossoming love affairs of young aristocrats, in the various great houses that they had served in, and gained enough practical experience of their own in the taverns and meeting halls which they frequented on their days off, no doubt.

Perhaps a little of their earthy, practical wisdom would help. But then, once again, she decided against it. They would not understand, and besides, it would be a great loss of decorum for the lady of the house to go to her own staff, begging them for amorous insights.

No, that course of action was simply out of the question.

There was really only one thing for it. She would have to be patient, and wait until next she saw Sterling by chance. There she could get a sense of how he felt, and how best she should approach their floundering love affair. And, as it happened, there was a ball scheduled for two days hence, at the Earl of Stanningfield's London residence... She steeled herself to endure the wait.

*

Perhaps predictably, Hemsbridge was not there. Lady Duckington consulted the tally that she had been compiling, somewhere at the back of her mind. That made it a whole week since last she had seen him. August was rumbling inevitably forward, and yet their affair had lost all momentum.

She was greeted with the customary cordiality by her hosts.

She had known Charles, the Earl, since shortly after her marriage, and they had pursued a brief but passionate love affair some six years ago, when he had been more in the habit of pursuing scandalous liaisons than settling down to happy marriages with schoolmistresses.

His wife she knew less well, owing to her previous lowly position within society, although she had always seemed polite and well-spoken. Looking at her now from afar, chatting confidently at the centre of a group of well-bred ladies, Lady Duckington regretted, a little, the cattier and more scathing remarks, that she and other society onlookers had made, when they had heard of the match. Blood, it seemed, trumped breeding, at least in this case, and Miss Catherine Thornberry had metamorphosed with grace and ease into the new role of Countess Stanningfield. Even her pregnancy, still only slight, but decidedly noticeable, beneath her finely tailored cream-yellow frock, did not dull this general impression.

"I see you are admiring my wife's glowing health, Amelia. We are both so happy that she is expecting" said Lord Stanningfield, appearing behind her suddenly, and placing his hand for a brief moment on her back. It gave her the barest tingle of pleasure, a reminder of their previous status as lovers. He was still as darkly handsome as ever, his powerful frame held tight beneath an elegant black suit, his thick dark hair framing his handsome features perfectly.

In the very recent past, Lady Duckington would have considered using her wiles to try and seduce him, married man or no, but, on this occasion, she was surprised to feel little desire for him.

He was undoubtedly desirable, yet she knew, instinctively, that her heart and mind were now engaged elsewhere - for now, at least, it seemed it was necessary that a man be Lord Hemsbridge, for him to command Amelia's affections.

"Indeed, my lord" she replied, returning him to formality. "It is most admirable how swiftly Lady Stanningfield has taken both to society, and to her marital duties."

"Well" he said, winking in the playful, almost schoolboyish manner he still occasionally adopted.

"I'd like to think that I had more than a little hand in both developments."

Amelia graced this masculine humour, with a gentle laugh. He still had his charms, there was no denying that.

"- and, I must confess, it brings me great satisfaction, the ease with which my beloved has dismissed all of the questions which society no doubt levelled at her character, on hearing of the match."

"Indeed? I cannot recall any such questions being brought to my attention. She is of the de Quincey line, is she not?"

"Yes, but don't pretend so with me, Lady Duckington. I think you and I are well-acquainted enough for me to say, in confidence, that, noble lineage or not, my wife was raised in a barely adequate cottage, and the aristocracy of England were all too aware of that fact, at the time of our betrothal."

"A betrothal which, as I recall, lasted all of five minutes, before culminating in an improvised marriage in a Suffolk church."

"My Lady's powers of recollection are, as ever, without peer. Now, I think it's only fitting, considering the history that we two share, for you and Lady Stanningfield to become better acquainted. My lady…" he said, beckoning for Catherine to come over. She made her excuses to her guests, and moved at once to her husband's side.

"My dear, I believe that you had the pleasure of meeting Lady Duckington, briefly, at our house party, not too long after we were wed, but have not seen her since?"

"I believe that to be the case, my Lord" said Lady Stanningfield, in a relaxed tone of voice, which suggested she was getting used to other women's jealousy and negativity. Their eyes met, both shades of piercing blue, and found in each other a surprising sense of holding a deep sadness, that only time and shared pain could unlock. Despite herself, and her usually dismissive manner towards socially well behaved ladies, Lady Duckington sensed that, in Catherine, she had met, perhaps, something of a kindred spirit.

She was quite certain that Catherine, between what she had seen of her at that house party (which Amelia rather winced to remember), and what the ladies of society had almost certainly had to say about her, knew very well how unpleasant and haughty Amelia had often been. Yet, in Catherine's eyes, she saw no sign of harsh judgement – a fact which profoundly shocked her.

"Well, I'll leave you two to get better acquainted" said Stanningfield, smoothly, in the manner of a host well-used to curating such meetings.

"Far beyond my powers to interfere in a conversation passed between two esteemed society ladies. You will excuse me..." he left the two women locked in each other's gaze.

"You are the wife of Lord Duckington, I understand?"

"Yes" replied Amelia, with a tone, which hinted at the guilt she felt, at the thought of her husband, trapped on his death bed out in the shires while she was carousing with the fashionable and beautiful here in London. Although Percival had bade her do just this, she could not but feel wrong about it.

"Though for how much longer, I dare not speculate. My Lord is unwell, and the physician fears his position could be terminal."

"It is, indeed, a great tragedy for us all." Catherine said, formally. She was getting more used to the tone of detachment high society required.

The English aristocracy, it seemed, could discuss an invading army battering down the doors of their own mansions, in the same cold and detached manner one might reserve for talking about cream tea or duck ponds. She enjoyed mimicking them.

"Yes, yes, you are right of course" said Amelia in reply, a little hint of exacerbation encroaching on her speech. "Although I have to admit, I have known, for many long years that this day would come, and that I would outlive my husband. I suppose it is all but inevitable, when one marries a gentleman nigh on four times one's age. It is sad, of course, but not unexpected, and..." she paused for a moment.

She found that she was on the point of discussing the innermost contents of her heart and mind.

It was rather risky and exposing, but she did continue to sense a certain kinship, as those somewhat disapproved of by society, between herself and Lady Stanningfield, a perception that could not be discounted. And the idea of speaking honestly with another woman was an unusual, and tempting, prospect.

"... well, if I might confide in my hostess the rather intimate feelings that such a development inspires...."

"Please do" said Catherine, in a tone that conveyed trust more than it did mere politeness.

"- then I might add that my husband's passing is not entirely unwelcome. For you see, fond as I am of him, and grateful for the comfort, nay luxury, that he has provided, I have never truly loved him, and my heart now belongs I believe, to another."

For a moment, Catherine glanced solemnly at the floor. This apparently evasive act at once gave Amelia some concern that she had rather overfaced herself, and revealed far too much, all at once, to a woman she had barely met before. *'What was I thinking?'* she thought, chastising herself.

She had, it seemed, perhaps made a fool of herself, desperate to confide in someone, to find some true friend, rather than one of the sycophantic bores she kept as acquaintances. But then, in a moment, all of those fears were dispelled, as Catherine raised her head and looked at her directly, warmth filling her big blue eyes.

"I can understand my lady's position entirely."

Catherine spoke in the friendly tone of conspiracy that she had learned from her mother in all those years of dreaming of a husband, in their cottage back in Suffolk.

"It cannot have been easy, sustaining a protracted marriage which had been, from the start, arranged from without, for the advancement of a family name and fortune, rather than for romance. I have no doubt that Lord Duckington has been a kind and gracious husband, but is almost certainly some way beyond being the sort of man a young girl dreams of being paired with." Amelia found herself nodding vigorously at this neat articulation of her feelings. It seemed that her judgement had been right! Catherine did understand, and sympathise with, her position, and how glorious it felt to at last be understood!

"You desire, I should imagine…" Lady Stanningfield continued "-some of the things that it is only natural for a woman to desire. Namely, a passionate connection, with a handsome and charming gentleman of appropriate age and rank, which brings some relief for one's anxieties and frustrations in the arms of one who truly cares and understands, and, dare I put it rather bluntly, a child, as the natural issue of such an affair. Am I correct in my evaluations?"

"Oh my lady!" gasped Amelia, with a gratitude so great she could not properly express it in words. "You cannot know how correct you are! Those are the real yearnings of my heart, the very wick at the centre of the candle of my heart, burning for such a love as you have described. I long for romance, and for the chance of a child." Amelia paused a moment, taking a steadying breath, encouraged by Catherine's open and caring expression.

"That chance has been too long in the coming, and as I advance in years I fear that, if it does not happen soon, it will be too late. I love a man, a suitable man who could make all of those things possible for me, yet…"

She stopped, almost physically overwhelmed by the weight of what she was next to say. For the first time in her adult life, she felt the prick of tears in her eyes – and at a public gathering, no less!

"- yet I worry, frantically, that my feelings are not fully reciprocated." Once again, her words of concern and confidence were met with a reassuring smile.

"You are a handsome woman, my Lady," Catherine said, "more so than most, as well as possessing certain virtues of intelligence, wit and insight. I have no doubt that, even if this proposed candidate for your affections proves to be inconstant and wavering, some other fellow will turn up, sooner rather than later, who might fill the void in your life." Lady Duckington felt like crying, and bouncing, in a most improper fashion, for joy, and embracing Catherine, this generous hearted soul, all at once. But, of course, she was able to do none of these things - for she was interrupted, at that very moment, by a footman, bearing a very grave expression and holding out to her a single sheet of paper.

"Lady Duckington" he said "- I am sorry to interrupt, but I'm afraid I must bring you tragic news. We have just received word that Lord Duckington has passed away at the Sussex property of his friend. Your man of business asks that you repair to Charingdon Hall at once. This note was enclosed with one to my master, asking that he convey the news to you, and offer you whatever assistance was needed."

"I shall go with all haste. Thank you, my good man." Lady Duckington spoke with the dignity that such tragic occasions demanded of a Lady of breeding.

The note confirmed what the footman had said, adding that Viscount Duckington's body would be brought, with haste, but all due care and respect, to his ancestral home at Charingdon Hall, so that he might be buried amongst the generations of his ancestors in the holy grounds of the small but beautiful parish church.

Bidding her regards to Catherine, and realising, with some disappointment, that it seemed Hemsbridge was, again, not going to make an appearance, she left the room to prepare for a trip to Charingdon Hall, in Surrey, on the morrow.

Chapter Fifteen

In idle moments throughout her decade of marriage to Lord Duckington, Amelia had, on occasion, imagined the reading of his will, his funeral, and the moment that she had always known would come, her step into freedom, with the receipt of her inheritance.

At especially low moments in the marriage, when she had felt bereft, and yearned for a younger, more virile man, to bring her the satisfaction that all parties knew the old Viscount could never deliver, fantasizing about it had brought her comfort.

At other times, assailed by guilt and a sort of resigned affection for the old duffer, it had been a sad thought to her, morbid even, bringing her a combination of sorrow and guilt.

Now the moment was here, and all she felt was numbness.

On the carriage drive south from London, through the rolling hills of Surrey, she had felt very little. A consciousness of this made her sad, dimly, but really it was a sense that she ought to feel more than she did, which dampened her otherwise acute sense of her feelings. She had gazed out onto the fields and hills, seen the trees still standing tall, swaying only very lightly in the breeze, and rather related herself to these stout bastions of nature. They didn't care what any human beings did, whether they lived or whether they died, and for now, rolling and bumping along country roads, neither did she. She was as cold and constant as the waves that buffeted England's southern shore, not changing for any man, least of all any husband.

She arrived at Charingdon Hall to find the staff just finishing laying out the Viscount in the formal Drawing Room.

Her feelings changed very abruptly when she saw his body. He looked little different from when she had visited him barely a week ago, somehow frozen in that moment in her mind and it struck her at once how little everything had changed. He was no long moving, his great gut, filled out from years of idleness and feasting, now diminished as illness had worn him away, did not heave up and down in time with his chest, but, otherwise, it was the same Viscount Duckington who greeted her, lifeless, dressed elegantly, and placed in his final bed – a coffin.

At first there was an unreality to it, as if she were simply dreaming an especially vivid dream, but then she was struck suddenly by pain and sadness, and cried. The tears brought her some relief, and made proceeding easier for the doctor, priest and lawyer who were in attendance.

These men were professionals in the field of death and were used to such reactions. It would have been rather awkward for all if the wife of the deceased had not shed gushing, spontaneous tears on seeing her dead husband, and on this occasion, Amelia could not help but oblige.

'Why am I crying?' she thought to herself, but realised rapidly that it was a foolish question. She had spent years in the company of this man, revealed to him many of her most intimate secrets, anxieties and fears. He had provided for her through thick and thin, in sickness and in health, and now death had parted them, at last. A warm and somehow comforting, even if only in the security that he had provided, presence had been removed from her life, and the lack of love (and utter lack of lust) she had felt for him through all these years, suddenly didn't seem to matter at all. She even (briefly) forgot about the Marquess of Hemsbridge, and instead sat, for an indeterminate stretch of time, which no-one felt any need to measure, by her husband's side, quietly sobbing.

At last her tears slowed sufficiently for the solicitor, Mr. Runciman, to propose moving elsewhere to discuss the will. She nodded seriously, picked herself up, accepted the handkerchief that the vicar had offered, and stepped next door.

*

The following day saw the formal culmination of all of this, in the actual reading of the will. She had been briefed accordingly by the family's lawyer, but he could not disclose the full details of her inheritance until all concerned parties were assembled for this most important, but depressing of ceremonies.

Aside from the doctor and vicar, who had dutifully volunteered to serve as witnesses, there were only two people in attendance, Lord Duckington's cousin and nominated heir, and his widow, Lady Duckington.

Duckington's cousin was a brisk and charmless man, who seemed extremely concerned, despite having been formally nominated when his relative was still alive, that somehow he was to be denied what he believed to be rightfully his.

And what he considered that to be was the full estate, including three smaller properties and various large estates, moveable riches in the form of jewellery, paintings, and other effects of varying degrees of worth, and a not inconsiderable monetary fortune, which the old man had been rather careful with over the years.

He cast worried sideways glances at the beautiful widow, as the solicitor shuffled his papers and prepared for the reading, here in the rather dark surrounds of the library at Charingdon Hall.

"I see that all concerned parties and the required witnesses are assembled. Excellent…" he said, after a lengthy clearing of his throat. He had a slow and resonant voice, rather unlike the sort of tone one associates with the legal profession. Amelia had expected brevity and quickness.

"This shouldn't take any longer than any of us might expect it to…"

"Well, get one with it man!" the cousin said, rather churlishly. "Some of us far better things to do than sit here and listen to you witter!"

"As my Lord desires... very well. The last will and testament of Percival Charingdon, Ninth Viscount Duckington, commences with all the usual legal niceties and necessary formalities, and then proceeds as such, *'to my dearly beloved wife Amelia, whom I have cherished and adored these past ten years of marriage and whose quite natural expectations of passionate romance I regret I have no doubt disappointed in my age and corpulence, I bequeath my house at Springden Chase, including relevant attached estates, and my London townhouse, as well as an annual income of £5,000 to be drawn from the London bank account which I have established for this purpose. I leave her, with all my love, such riches as I can, in order to enable her to live the life of comfort and pleasure which she has been accustomed to.'*

Amelia blushed. This was considerably more than she had expected! She knew that she was to receive enough money to live decently off, but to have Springden and a little land as well was quite something! Truly, she would miss the generosity of spirit Lord Duckington had always shown her. He had known, no doubt, of her frequent infidelities and brittle nature, but it seemed to have affected his feelings for her very little.

'The remainder of my estates and worldly wealth, additional to those properties entailed to my title...' the slow-speaking lawyer continued *'I leave to my dear cousin Mr. Albert Percival Redmayne Esquire, whom I believe to be my only surviving blood relative. As such, he will be the new Viscount Duckington. May he derive satisfaction from his inheritance, and preserve the good name and honour of the House of Charingdon for future generations to come.'*

"I must protest!" exclaimed Redmayne, rising to his feet. "I was led to believe I was to get the lot! What has this hussy done to deserve Springden Chase and such a generous annual income!"

"My Lord," the solicitor spoke tersely - he was used to aggrieved relatives getting angry over wills, but this aggressive demonstration of misplaced expectation of entitlement was rather perturbing, even to an experienced professional such as himself. "- it is not in my purview to divine the motivations of the deceased. Lord Duckington was most scrupulous in the preparation of his last will and testament, and I must inform you that the document is sound and legally binding. Now if that is all, then our business here is concluded and we may adjourn."

"Bah!" Redmayne shouted. "Tommy rot! The old bugger always had an eye for a pretty bit of skirt. I'm not happy about this Runciman!" He stormed out, and Lady Duckington concluded that she would not be disappointed if she never saw him again.

Mr Runciman, embarrassed, apologised to her for Redmayne's vulgar language, wiping his brow with a handkerchief, and arranged for her to visit his offices the following week, to view and sign all of the required papers, to finalise the transfer of ownership.

*

The funeral was a sedate and sparsely attended affair. Really, at this stage, it felt like a token formality. All legal issues had been resolved, and Lord Duckington had been old and infirm for some time.

Those of his friends who survived made a dutiful appearance, demonstrating only a little grief, and not expecting much in the way of a wake. Despite all of this, however, Amelia found that she was still sad enough to shed a few fresh tears, at the sombre dignity of the funeral carriage, the grand claims of the vicar's words, and the stately descendent of the very wide coffin into its eternal resting place.

The newly widowed Lady Duckington received the good wishes of the small congregation, and retired to her bed in a coaching inn just outside Hastings. She had arranged the removal of all of her personal effects from Charingdon Hall with some haste, sending them on to the London townhouse that was now hers, and refused to spend another night in Charingdon Hall, not wishing to be beholden to the new Viscount Duckington in any way whatsoever.

Sleep eluded her for some time. Grief nagged at her in the background, but really, what was exercising her mind was a seemingly endless succession of thoughts about her future, and what it could possibly hold. She feared that, without a husband to provide her what she truly desired, it was quite possible that love, passion, emotional fulfilment and, of course, children, might elude her forever.

An image of Sterling Asterwood, Marquess Hemsbridge, rose in her mind. It had reached a point, she admitted to herself, where her desires were not simply focussed on finding a man to provide her desires, but had become completely locked on the idea of that man being Sterling. He simply had to be hers. She could imagine no other man creating these thoughts and feelings in her.

She felt new emotions, new depths of attachment into which she was descending. Could this be love?

And…. What if their rift could not be mended? What if he chose never to see her again? What would she do? It was not to be contemplated!

Sighing deeply and thinking a little despairingly, of him, she finally drifted off to sleep.

*

Sitting in Mr Runciman's office a few days later, Amelia gasped with shock as she heard the fine detail of the conditions under which she had been granted this inheritance. It was not so simple and straightforward as it had sounded. Not at all.

Two terrible conditions attended upon her ownership of the two properties, and failing to meet either of them would see the properties, and a portion of her income, pass to the new Viscount. She looked at Mr Runciman in horror, as he explained

"My Lady, I am most sorry to tell you of this, but your husband insisted – he felt that, in the long term, these conditions would ensure you a happy future, more so than any other option."

He nodded, looking uncomfortable, and continued.

"He was most concerned that a Lady, enjoying her life, would not have the time to spend on maintaining the two properties, and might neglect one of them. He could not bear the thought of one falling into disrepair. But, equally, he, could not bear the thought of you immersing yourself in dry bookwork and estate management – he wanted you to have the chance at a life he had not been able to give you."

Amelia, nodded, wondering exactly what this tangle would result in.

"The two conditions are as follows:

1. That, should you be too long away from either property, the property less attended, should pass, automatically, to the ownership of the new Viscount Duckington. And should this happen, a proportion of your income will also pass to him, as support for the property. This condition only to apply until such time as the second condition is fulfilled.

2. That, should you not marry, within the year after his lordship's death, your mourning period notwithstanding, both properties will pass to the new Viscount, and you will be left with no property, and very little money. Once you marry, within that year, these conditions will become void, and the properties and the income will be yours, unconditionally.

It was his Lordship's belief that the only way you would be happy in the long term, was to marry again, to a younger man, who could give you the children that he never could. It was his opinion that the properties and income would provide you a dowry, and a chance to ensure that you would never want."

Amelia simply sat. The implications rolled through her mind, and left her feeling more powerless than she ever had in her life. She could not countenance losing either property, and yet, surely that might come to pass, as, nowhere had it been specified how long an absence might be 'too long'. Equally, she could not countenance the thought of marrying in haste, simply to ensure her survival – for who would she marry?

It was, however, obvious to her that she must, somehow, find someone to marry, for she refused to lose all that she had been given. She also refused to tie herself to a man that she did not care for, to place herself in another loveless marriage.

The thought of potentially spending the rest of her life in such a state was like ashes in her mouth, like the destruction of all that she thought she had gained. She must think on this with utmost concentration – for a solution must be found, and found fast.

Chapter Sixteen

After three weeks away from London, Sterling had to admit to himself that he was glad to be back in the capital. He had spent that three weeks sorting out the mess that MacGregor had created for him, hiring a new estate manager, visiting all of the tenants to reassure them, drawing up a plan for returning the estate, and all of the tenant cottages as well, to the condition that they should have been maintained in, in the first place.

It had been satisfying, but rather exhausting.

He usually liked the countryside and what it offered, the serenity, the peace, the opportunities for games and hunting, and the refuge from the prying eyes of old hens and meddling gossips. But he was still a young man, still brimming with energy and confidence and life, and for the young, a city like London had an almost magnetic attraction.

The largest, grandest, and most prosperous city in the world, if one had a little money and a lot of energy, it had enough to keep one amused for more than a lifetime.

One particular attraction that the city held for him was the possibility of seeing Amelia once again. He knew, or at least, felt sure that he knew, that he might find her there, at her townhouse or engaging in clever, if rather barbed, conversation at balls, looking for trouble away from her ailing husband. Having not seen her in the weeks since their altercation, he had no knowledge of her husband's condition, or of the need for her to be mourning him and settling her affairs after his tragic passing. As a consequence, his mind turned to what he hoped would be an energetic, and thoroughly satisfying, reconciliation between them.

On arriving at his West End townhouse, always a comforting *pied a terre* in the city, which many poorer folk called 'the great smoke', he had business to attend to, before he might be free to indulge in any amorous pursuits. As ever, when a busy gentleman, with estates to administer, arrives in a residence he has not been at for some time, there were many letters awaiting him. The vast majority were tedious, bills and the like, correspondences about land management, about tenants and rates of rent and other things which he knew to be important, but preferred to leave to his hired men of business.

One letter however, immediately stood out. It had somehow got lost in amongst all of this more humdrum and commercially focused mail, but was unmistakably addressed in a more personal capacity, wrapped in a fine parchment envelope and bearing a noble seal.

His heart fluttered slightly at the thought that it might be from Amelia, and he was overcome, once more, with a longing to apologise for snapping at her when last they met. Tearing the letter open, he devoured its contents greedily.

It was to disappoint him. The letter was not, as he had hoped, written in Amelia's own, gracefully flowing, hand, but, rather, in the more prim and formal writing of her butler. It informed him briskly that Lady Duckington had had to urgently convey herself to Charingdon Hall in Surrey, to attend to the funeral of her husband, who had now passed away, and from whom she had received some, apparently substantial, inheritance. It expressed her expectation that they might meet again soon, as her mourning, and other matters permitted, but did not say when and, perhaps most frustratingly, gave no indication of how long a period of mourning Amelia planned to follow.

The letter's initial effect was almost painful. Sterling had not entirely realised, before receiving it, what such a correspondence would mean to him. He had wished to see Amelia again, certainly. She was an attractive woman after all, and he had no wish to see their most stimulating affair brought to a halt any time soon. They had always got on well and found each other attractive, in the narrowest sense of that word, he had mainly assumed.

He had felt certain that his longing to apologise was merely based on an unwillingness to see it all come crashing down, and out of a gentlemanly wish to right the wrongs he knew he had inflicted upon her, through his crass and arrogant behaviour. Now however, he realised, with a jolt, that he had developed stronger feelings than all of that suggested.

Now he feared, he might just be falling, more than a little, for Lady Amelia Duckington.

His thoughts moved forward rapidly, as they are wont to do in these situations. The initial sting of disappointment was replaced by a most exhilarating rush of hope, and a sense of fresh possibility. For, he realised, once she had recovered from the death of her husband (which, he calculated, would cause her only the sorrow required of a young widow, and no more, owing to their limited attachment and considerable disparity in age) she was now a free woman, and he a free man.

The eligible bachelor and the grief-stricken widow might form a quite natural pairing, especially considering the fact that they were already known to have something of an attachment to one another.

Why, now that she had inherited property and wealth in her own right, she might even be a match his mother would approve of! Sterling found himself grinning like a small boy. Perhaps things were working themselves out at last!

*

The next few balls were to prove disappointing. Hemsbridge had set himself up for a fall. Unlike in the past, where he had attended reluctantly, at his mother's insistence, and could therefore detach himself from the experience accordingly, now he arrived every time full of hope and enthusiasm, only to see all of that smashed.

He would enter ball rooms bright-eyed and positive, only to look around at the assembled faces, and see that the one face he wished to see was not there.

He would make thorough surveys of every possible room in the house, annoying more than a few loyal footmen, suspicious of his poking his nose into odd corners, but could never seem to find what he was looking for.

It was, he supposed, foolish of him to expect her to attend, so soon after her husband's death – to do so would quite be flouting convention – but then, she had ever been willing to do exactly that.

Finally, he generally ended up on the peripheries of other's conversations, or took to smoking alone on outdoor terraces.

"I don't know what on earth has come over you, my boy" said his mother, ruefully.

"Why, it would once have required a regiment of cavalry to get you to as many balls as you seem to want to go to these days, and yet when we actually get here you're just as sulky as you ever were. More so, dare I say it, though I hadn't previously thought it to be possible. Whatever can be the matter with you?"

"It's none of your concern mother" he said, trying to avoid being dragged into a lengthy and painful examination of these unfamiliar feelings which he was struggling to manage.

"Need I remind you that I am a grown man? I manage my estates and my own affairs, with no-one else's input. If only you could invest in me the same trust with respect to matters of the heart, as you do with respect to agricultural matters, then we might both be more contented."

"Good lord you've become arrogant of late!" she snapped, taking none of his sentiment lying down.

"If only your father were here to see this. He'd have knocked all of this romantic, self-regarding nonsense clean out of you, with his boots on if necessary! What on earth is wrong with Lady Priscilla Woldingham, eh? Or Lady Arabella Edington, for that matter? Very eligible girls, both of them, wonderful dowries! Why can't you find it in yourself to make peace and settle down with one of them, eh?"

"Mother, we have been over this conversation more times than I can possibly keep track of. I've told you, I'm not interested in any of these fey little heiresses you keep rustling up for me! They bore me beyond words - I want something more!"

"More?! Rot! If everyone were like you, always demanding 'more' the human race would have died out long ago. Sometime, soon, you'll know that I'm right. You'll realise there's more important things in life than your precious feelings."

"I eagerly await the day" Sterling snapped, sarcastically. He knew that his mother suspected that what was really exercising him, was thoughts of Lady Duckington, but she wouldn't ever let on. To acknowledge it would be too painful for her, too complicated, for, to even admit that Lady Duckington might be someone he cared for, represented the loss of all hope for her dearly held dynastic plans. They stood there in stony silence as he stubbed out his cigarillo and made to summon the carriage to go home.

Chapter Seventeen

Not very far away at all, in another west London townhouse, Amelia was also growing restless. She was being bothered incessantly, not by a mother (hers had passed some years ago) but by a suitor, namely her late husband's cousin, the new Viscount Duckington. Mr Redmayne, as he had, until very recently, been known, was a persistent fellow, full of new energy and determination after inheriting such an impressive estate and title, after languishing for years in obscurity in the shires, and on his small estate in Scotland. He appeared to think that, even after his totally insulting behaviour at the reading of her husband's will, she should find his suit acceptable.

He had a strange hybrid accent which Amelia simply could not warm to, and yet it was his personality, already adequately demonstrated by that behaviour, more than anything else, that completely deterred her affections.

He pressed and needled away, without grace, wit or charm. He was not entirely unhandsome, but any positive effect his looks might possess was more or less negated by his manner. She knew, and was amazed that he should believe she did not, that the only reason he wished to marry her, was to get under his control that part of her late husband's fortune and properties which had been left to Amelia. It seemed that he was aware of the conditions of her late husband's will, and saw them as an excellent opportunity to have a beautiful woman in his bed, as well as control of the properties.

He thought that he had her trapped, and that she would, sooner rather than later, bow to the inevitable, and accept his proposal. He saw her rejection of him as wilful stubbornness.

Her opinion did not matter in the least, to him. His primary motivation in life appeared to be simple greed.

"Well?" he exclaimed one day, as she was trying to relax and enjoy a cup of tea.

"When are we getting married then, Duckers?" he had seen fit to bestow this nickname upon her, entirely against her will, and she found it entirely alienating. She had never been called 'Duckers' in all her life. It was the sort of stupid name men gave each other at school, or in raucous clubs when they were smoking and drinking together. She thought it most improper.

"Need I remind you, my Lord" she replied, struggling with all her might to contain her rage. "That I am in mourning for my late husband, and not in a suitable position to entertain your, ..." she looked at him, doing everything she could to convey her distaste through her narrowed eyes and pursed lips "... your rather crudely expressed suggestions."

It did no good. For weeks now, it had done no good at all. He had called on her endlessly, seeming to presume that, as the successor to her husband's title, he was the logical candidate to claim her in marriage, to bring the estate back together. He would insist on interpreting her distaste as flirtation, and her protestation as evidence that he was getting through. It was unbearable. She was seriously considering refusing to see him, ever again. But.... then what might he do?

"Ha! Stuff and nonsense. That's not what I've heard said of you out in the clubs." He came and sat down beside her, pressing his face close to hers, invading her space. It would appear that he had simply no idea how to behave around a grieving widow, or, indeed, any woman, for that matter.

"I've heard the chaps say you're quite the goer, if you know what I mean. Likes it on the fast flat tracks, like all the finest runners and riders, if you catch my drift, what!"

"Your metaphor remains, opaque, my Lord." Her voice was icy enough to freeze a substantial lake, but he simply ignored it, again.

"They've all had a go, haven't they? Wedding ring didn't deter you! Aldercott, Renley, Tarringsworth, they've all had a turn in the Lady Duckington saddle, I hear! And now that I'm the rightful inheritor, I think I'm rather owed a go myself! You have to marry, so, take the easy path – marry me."

He grabbed hold of her, roughly, and tried to kiss her. She wrenched herself to the side, just in time to prevent contact between his slobbering mouth and her delicate cheek.

Redmayne's one saving grace was that he knew when to withdraw, and did not seek to physically impose himself any further. She did not have much confidence that such restraint would remain the case, if he continued his pursuit of her much longer. And he would, for, to him, she was nothing more than a convenient bedwarming bonus, which came with the properties he wanted.

"Hmmph" he exclaimed, rising to his feet and straightening his dress coat. "Have it your way, for now. But, know that I shall receive what is rightfully mine, one way or another. I know women and their ways, and I know what I'm owed, and as my father always told me, any Redmayne worth their salt knows what they're owed. Good day, my Lady."

He took himself off, and she breathed a huge sigh of relief on hearing the door shut firmly behind him. From the resounding nature of the sound, she could see that her staff held the new Viscount in as little favour as she did. The staff were, however, not aware of those two conditions on the will – she had chosen not to inform them, feeling that her worries were not for her staff to know of.

Lady Duckington's junior chambermaid, Mary, had been loitering in the hallway, eavesdropping on the whole sorry scene. She had seen her mistress at all moments, high and low, noble and less virtuous, over the last 10 years, and now she could not but feel a pang of sympathy. *'The poor lady!'* she thought.

The earth had barely been laid on her husband's grave and already she had this man, who was an imbecile, new Viscount or not, coming round trying, with all the grace of a lame ox, to woo her.

It was horrible, and, although the Lady had not always been the kindest employer, and had frequently scandalized everyone belowstairs with some of her fruitier outbursts against acquaintances and relatives, she knew, at once, that in this instance, she had to show Lady Duckington some kindness. Smoothing back her dark hair, she entered the drawing room.

"If it please you m'Lady" she said, speaking directly to her employer, woman to woman, for the first time. She was deeply conscious of her rough accent, cockney and harsh, like the dockers of the east end, and not befitting a grand drawing room in one of the finest residences of the nobility.

However, the eyes that turned to meet her were not critical or unwelcoming, but rather sad, and soft, and seeming to beckon her in to say her piece.

Lady Duckington looked almost as if she had been about to cry, though, realising that she was not alone caused her instinctively to suppress her emotion, stiffen her posture, and receive young Mary with dignity.

"Yes?" she asked, curious.

"Well, not wishing to speak out of place my Lady, and knowing that I'm rather a junior member of your household, I just wanted to say that you have all our sympathies miss, I mean, my Lady."

Lady Duckington was rather taken aback. However, rather than snapping at the girl, as she would have done and, perhaps, even should have done, considering their respective stations, she instead moved to entertain what it was the simple serving girl had to say.

Unguarded and fragile as she was, her usual layers of haughtiness and affectation had peeled off, and she was quietly glad of a little human contact.

"Whatever do you mean girl?" she said.

"Well, we've all… that is, all of who work under your roof, my lady, we've seen that new Viscount Duckington, the young gentleman, round here, and I have to say, we disapprove of his conduct. It ain't right or proper, as my old Mum would have said, for him to be imposing his'self on a Lady, just after she's been bereaved, like. Not respecting of his Lordship's last wishes neither, god rest his soul."

The expected reaction, society's reaction, would have been for Lady Duckington to rise to her feet, express her disgust at the insolence of this chambermaid, seeking to offer her opinion on the private affairs of her employer, and then have her dismissed immediately from the staff.

But Lady Duckington could not have been more grateful for the honesty, and indeed, the courage, of the girl, and instead, smiled warmly, and, for the first time in her life, offered words of genuine kindness to one of her social inferiors.

"Thank you…. Mary, is it? I appreciate your kindness, and you may further convey my gratitude to the rest of the staff, if that is indeed, how they feel as well. His Lordship's conduct has been rather burdensome these past weeks, and it is gratifying to have the good wishes of my household. Thank you once again."

"That's quite alright, my Lady, sorry to have disturbed you."

"Not at all." Mary took her leave, and Lady Duckington unfurled a silk handkerchief with which to dry her unaccountably damp eyes.

*

She did all that she could in the subsequent days to avoid thinking of Sterling. It was unhelpful, and improper, for a widow to be fixating on her lover, one of her lovers, so soon after her husband's death, yet she could not seem to avoid it. Try as she might, he had undeniably burrowed his way into her consciousness and could not seem to be shifted. And, with each thought of him, came the little, wishful, shimmer of the idea, that, perhaps, he might be someone she could marry. Marrying a man like Sterling would not be so terrible.....

But... after her harsh words to him, upon their last meeting, she must be brutally honest with herself – it seemed unlikely that he wished to see her again, let alone marry her. It was more likely that he had seen her, as had so many before him, as simply an easy path to a bit of physical relief, and had now, in the face of her sharp tongue, chosen to move on. It would explain why she had not heard from him for some time. But still, he persisted in her mind.

She would be saying her morning prayers for her husband and Hemsbridge would be there in her mind, flashing images of him, of his handsome face grinning at her, of his thick hair pressed against her face, of his finely sculpted body pressed close against hers. Having never been a deeply pious woman, and knowing few of the prayers she felt she ought to recite, her prayers were short, and rather perfunctory.

Her duty done, she would rise to her feet, and allow the hot, physical presence of Sterling Asterwood to fill her thoughts, raising a tingling warmth in her body, reminding her of past pleasures, which, she could only hope, might be repeated again.

She would be taking tea in her study and sorting through some letters, and she would imagine Sterling there, with her, and then her mind would wander, and instead of concentrating on the affairs of her estate, or these polite correspondences from acquaintances, she would find herself day-dreaming, fantasising as to what Sterling might write to her, what richly textured romantic words he would have for her, should he ever forgive her their altercation, enough to write.

And then she would feel a great sadness, and be conscious of the yawning chasm his absence had left in her life, so much greater than the loss even of her husband. It made her feel anxious, and alone, and cut off, powerless in the universe, and suddenly she would find herself unable to drink her tea, unable to read her letters, unable to think clearly at all, and she would have to sit down and try to regain her sense.

She was not, in any way, used to feeling powerless, or to not knowing what it was that she might be doing, in the days ahead. Those conditions on the will simply exacerbated the feeling of powerlessness, and she could not forgive herself, for having alienated the only man whom she might have considered as a solution to the problem that the will created.

She longed for someone to share her troubles, to support her, for a human touch as firm and meaningful as Sterling's.

She would find herself reminded of it everywhere, at the most improper moments, when her maid, Brigitte, laced up her bodice. As the butler brushed past her shoulder as he was serving her at table. And, especially, in the comparison inevitably raised in her mind by the disgusting rough caresses of Albert Redmayne when he saw fit to insinuate himself into her life, always forcing his way past her staff and never giving her any notice. His certainty that he would have her as wife wore her down, and the dark despair of her plight left her isolated and despondent.

She could not stand him, and yet, cooped up like this, mourning and reminiscing, going over and over the damned will conditions in her mind, cut off from social life, company, gentlemen and the pleasures that they could all too easily bring, she found herself momentarily tempted, more than once, to surrender to his pathetic advances, if only for the fleeting satisfaction it might bring. The idea horrified her, almost as much as the marriage he kept casually proposing, and which such a physical union might inevitably engender, for surely, were she so foolish, he would use it to force their marriage, no matter the scandal.

She resolved that she must do something, anything, to bring relief from this terrible situation, to get away and escape. She remembered Springden Chase, the second part of her inheritance, out in Berkshire, a property that the will required her to visit often, not far from London, but far enough that she might be undisturbed there. Yes! As a solution, that seemed perfect. She could meet that condition of the will, and there, for a time at least, she could be a silent, grieving widow, read her books, ignore her letters, and oversee some improving work to the house and grounds.

She could throw herself into a private and well-organised life, away from all of this distraction and temptation, all of these reminders, at least for a while. She made her arrangements, bid her formal farewells by letter, and headed out to the country without further ado.

A fortnight later, Sterling received a letter, marked with the instantly recognizable stamp of the House of Charingdon, the family into which Lady Duckington had married. He was surprised, and pleasantly, for he had not heard from Amelia in some time.

Their correspondence had more or less broken down and their lives split off into separate compartments, hers the grieving widow picking her way through her own affairs, his, the bored bachelor, being hounded towards some loveless match or another by the demands of his mother, on the one hand, and high society on the other.

He had, by force of will, stopped himself from regularly thinking of Amelia, of the bond they shared and the intimacy that they had enjoyed, but the sight of her postmark brought a heady rush of feelings which he had not entirely anticipated.

It was not just a low, physical longing he felt, though that was certainly part of the picture, but also a desire to be close to her, to feel her, to press his hand into hers and take in all that was hers, body and spirit. It was a quite overwhelming feeling.

The letter sadly, was not from Amelia. The two had not corresponded for a while, and that layer of frost did not yet appear to have thawed. It was in fact, again from her butler, and was addressed to him directly.

My dearest Lord Hemsbridge, it began.

Please accept, in advance, my apologies for communicating with you in so direct and unprecedented a manner, but circumstances, I fear, demand hasty and unorthodox action. Hemsbridge stopped reading for a moment. What on earth did the old fellow mean?

As you may be aware from following the society pages, Lord Duckington was recently, tragically lost to us, and this house passed to his widow, with whom you are of course, acquainted. The remainder of his estate, excepting some monies and a house in Surrey at Springden Chase (which were also for my Lady), passed to Albert Percival Redmayne, the new Viscount Duckington, who has been a regular visitor, though an often unexpected, and always unwelcome, one, here in Burton Lane. He has harassed my Lady in a most inappropriate manner for some weeks now, with incessant marriage proposals (most improper for a recently widowed woman in her fragile condition) and even physical advances of a most improper nature, which she has most definitely found extremely unwelcome.

The idea of this immediately incensed Hemsbridge.

He felt a hot rage course through him, to the extent where he actually gnashed his teeth together, and thought of Lady Duckington's honour. "The cad!" he exclaimed aloud, the idea of the Redmayne imbecile quickly turning his mood sour. He read on.

At any rate, his conduct has forced my lady to retire, perhaps indefinitely, to the countryside, at rather short notice and with only a very small staff to attend her. We have not had word yet from Springden Chase in Berkshire, where she had planned to go, and I fear her mood is a black one.

At this, Hemsbridge's emotions quickly switched from anger to sympathy, touched with more than a little fear for Amelia. Rather than imagining his fist connecting with the face of this Redmayne buffoon, he now thought of Amelia, and of his newfound desire to hold her, comfort her. Generally, when he thought of ladies his emotion was either annoyance or lust, but it was refreshing, if somewhat confusing, to feel this swelling warmth towards Amelia Duckington.

In the absence of my Lady, the new Viscount Duckington has laid claim to this house, citing his lawful status as inheritor of Lord Duckington's estates, and my Lady's absence, and some clause in the will, as just cause for title to the property to be given to him, even though this house was left to my Lady. Neither myself, nor any other members of staff here, being trained in the legal arts, and all of us lacking the authority to challenge a man of his breeding and title directly, I am writing to you in an appeal for aid. My Lady requires your assistance and that of her lawyer, Mr. Runciman, with some urgency.

In light of the rather delicate nature of events here, I propose, my Lord, that we meet in private on some neutral ground. I am familiar with a public house, not far from either of our residences, off Great Portland Street, 'The Lamb and Flag' where we could meet discreetly to discuss matters. I would recommend that your Lordship take what precautions are necessary to disguise your identity. I trust I shall see you there, at nine this evening.

Yours humble servant,

Herbert Jenkins,

Butler

The letter stirred something in Sterling, some instinct to protect, first and foremost, but also a strong need to know where he stood with Amelia. This was as good an opportunity as any for him to involve himself in Lady Duckington's affairs, and in so doing, know something more of the possibilities of their affair, of what she felt and whether there was any future between then. 'Yes' he thought, half-formed romantic notions developing in the back of his mind *'this is the answer! If Amelia has any doubts about seeing me again, surely, if I demonstrate the depth of my passion by assisting in casting off this rotter Redmayne, she will forgive me that altercation.'* Action was, he thought, rather easier than attempting quiet explanation... Seizing the letter decisively, he began preparations for an evening excursion...

*

Wearing a battered old great coat he'd borrowed from his coachman, and a modest black hat he had used to appear inconspicuous in the past, Sterling instructed his cab driver to drop him on Great Portland Street.

He knew this particular avenue well enough; it was one of upper class London's most handsome and notable thoroughfares, and he picked his way along it quietly in the evening gloom, past fashionable jewellers and haberdashers that served the nobility, and elegant townhouses, most of them built in the previous century.

Once he stepped off the main road, and into the side alley that Jenkins had mentioned in his note, however, he was in unfamiliar territory.

Not only did he not know the physical layout of these streets, but there was also an atmosphere that was unfamiliar and discomforting to him, an ambience of poverty and distress. An angry old woman asked him if he had any 'pretty pennies', and he did his best to ignore her for fear of having his pocket picked, or revealing to prying eyes that he had money. He was passed by a man in tattered clothing, who stank of gin and seemed to be hardly bothered to conceal a cudgel on his person, and was then growled at by a mangy dog, before the beast was called inside by its owner, snarling in a dense cockney idiom "gnasher! Get in 'ere!"

Sterling chuckled at the thought of his mother seeing him in such run-down surrounds. She would no doubt be scandalized, and shocked, and filled with fear. Bracing himself, he pushed on, and then into the 'Lamb and Flag' a modest looking inn with smoke spilling out of the chimney.

The tavern was half empty, which Sterling was quite glad of. A few harmless looking old men supped beer by the fire, and a younger, very lean fellow was enquiring as to the price of whisky at the bar.

Sterling immediately spotted Jenkins, where he sat in the opposite corner - he too was wearing consciously inconspicuous garb, and subtly beckoned him over with a raise of the eyebrows.

He had been joined by another man, a similarly gaunt and sombre looking professional, who he did not believe he had seen before.

"'My Lord" Jenkins said, barely raising his voice above a whisper "Might I convey my gratitude that you could come. This good gentleman is Mr. Runciman, attorney at law, who serves as Lady Duckington's solicitor, and was executor of the late Lord Duckington's will and testament."

"A pleasure, my Lord" offered Runciman, extending his hand.

"Likewise" muttered Sterling, accepting the proffered handshake. He could not prevent a suspicious expression finding its way onto his features.

"I am sorry that we had to meet in such unorthodox surrounds" continued Runciman, detecting the Marquess' scepticism. "Regrettably, developments require it. In fact, we have fallen into such a crisis that I'm afraid we had no other options."

"Do please explain what you mean" said Sterling, dispensing with formality as he was wont to do.

"Regrettably," Runciman continued in his lawyerly way "- Mr. Redmayne, who, as the closest living male relative, is Lord Duckington's heir, has invoked a clause in Lord Duckington's will, whereby a prolonged absence on the part of her Ladyship from either of the residences she inherited can lead to their passing automatically to him."

"What?!" cried Sterling, to the consternation of the other tavern-goers.

"I did try to talk the old Viscount out of that condition, but he was worried about either property passing into disrepair. And that's not the worst of it!" Runciman shook his head sadly

"The old Viscount was of the opinion that Lady Duckington should have the happiness that he had been unable to provide her – that of children. So he added a further clause to the will – that she must marry within a year of his death, or both properties, and most of her income, will pass to the new Viscount. The new Viscount feels that Lady Duckington, being now a widow, still possessed of some youth, but advancing in age, should be happy with that idea, and that he, as the inheritor, should be the logical candidate for her to marry. I feel that he acts simply from a desire to have in his control the entirety of the old Lord's estate, and rather than simply wait the year, and see what happens, risking her marrying someone else, he wants to get a bonus on the side, so to speak, of having a desirable woman as part of the bargain. He is using the condition about the houses as leverage, to force a rapid conclusion to the matter."

Mr Runciman looked most thoroughly disgusted at the whole thing.

"He says, to summarise, that unless she relents and marries him, he will claim the house, and with it, a considerable portion of her income, leaving her to Springden Chase in rural Berkshire, and something approaching penury. Which situation will only worsen, unless she marries by the end of the stipulated year, regardless."

"But this is outrageous! How on earth can he get away with such caddish behaviour!"

"Unfortunately the will is quite clear. Lord Duckington was keen for his bride to find another husband of suitable estates and wealth to keep her in the manner to which she was accustomed. He was terribly fond of her, you see, and only desired her happiness. Unfortunately however, as the terms of the will rested so heavily on this proposed condition, Redmayne has found something of a loophole. His Lordship did not specify how long 'a prolonged absence' was to be, and I, I am ashamed to admit, did not notice the omission. So the new Viscount has chosen to interpret 'prolonged' as a somewhat shorter timeframe than I would think reasonable, on top of the fact that he can claim both houses if she remains unmarried beyond a year from the old Viscount's death. He is greedy, I am sad to say, and wants this resolved in his favour, now."

"Damned dishonourable stuff sir!" Sterling said, feeling his blood boil. A huge part of him wanted to rush over to the house now and challenge this Redmayne idiot, the new Viscount Duckington, to a duel. Perhaps five years ago he would have, but, seeing the concerned faces of the two gentlemen before him, and thinking all at once of his beloved Amelia, he focussed his mind, and, considered his position.

"This is why we are appealing to you, my Lord" said Jenkins, interjecting. He had been nursing a pint of ale, clearly seeking some comfort in a drink.

"I know that, in a direct sense, this is no business of yours, but I fear that, for all of our sakes, it falls to you to intervene. You are, if I may speak plainly, the only man that has shown any sign of truly caring for her Ladyship, beyond her old husband, and she certainly appears to feel more for you than for any other, though she would most likely not admit it. Lady Duckington must return to London post-haste, and arrange a formal schedule of visits to the two properties, which Mr Runciman, as her solicitor, and the executor, can certify, to meet the conditions of the will. If this can be arranged, it will provide some time for her to attempt to address the marriage condition, without being forced to marry that cad, and then this sorry business might come to an end."

"You're quite right Jenkins." Sterling said, hastily. "It's time something was done about this. Gentlemen, we shall assemble at the house in two days' time, after I have retrieved Lady Duckington from Surrey. Mr Runciman, please draw up whatever papers will be needed. Then we shall settle matters once and for all with this Redmayne blighter, man to man. God speed!" They shook hands firmly, and went off in their separate directions into the London night.

*

Amelia, unaware of the drama unfolding in London, was finally beginning to feel more capable of clear thought, as the weeks away from Redmayne had given her some time to contemplate what she might do.

She had also quite fallen in love with Springden Chase, a property that she had only visited once before, for a very short time. It made her all the more determined to resolve the complex situation in her own favour.

She took long walks in the grounds, she sat for long hours in thought, and concluded, after all of that, that there was, truly, only one possible answer to the situation, which she could accept with a whole heart. Simply put, she must marry Sterling Asterwood, Marquess Hemsbridge, if she were ever to be happy again.

That left the not inconsiderable issue of the fact that she did not, at this point in time, know the truth of his feelings with respect to her. And she had no way, that she could think of, to ascertain what he thought, and felt. Perhaps, in the end, she would have to behave scandalously, and take herself, in person, to his house, to make her apologies for their argument, and see if, perhaps, she had any hope at all of his affections.

Chapter Nineteen

Fired by a passionate sense of the injustice of it all, Sterling did not bother waiting for a carriage to be prepared. Instead he arose early, not requiring Holbrook to rouse him, saddled Toulon, his finest horse, and galloped off, down the King's road and out of London, heading for Berkshire and the countryside, and, hopefully, the resolution of his emotional turmoil.

He had consulted a map the previous evening and it had confirmed him in his suspicions. He knew where Springden Chase was already. He had visited it as a young boy, and indeed been entertained there by the late Lord Duckington, who as memory served, had been considerably more erudite and energetic at that time than during his acquaintance with his wife. The house was a handsome manor in some lightly wooded country, just to the east of Reading. A stiff ride, which he knew Toulon to be more than capable of enduring, would surely carry him there in a matter of hours.

As he rode the passions assailing his mind switched from fury towards something rather more sentimental. He was pleased to be heading in the direction of Amelia, her gorgeously proportioned body, but also her smile, her touch, her laughter at his jokes and the constant, meandering witty conversations they had shared.

Her absence had gone on too long, he yearned for her, and could feel that yearning rising within him, not just an arousal of the body, but one of the heart. It shocked him, in a way, for he had never felt quite like this about a woman before.

The warmth of his thoughts kept him going, as he covered the miles at a fast and steady pace. When Toulon rounded a corner sharply, he perceived a large, elegant house, framed by poplar trees. He breathed deeply, taking it in, as he rode down the tree lined drive towards the front door.

He was greeted by a ridiculously old footman, who had clearly been holding the fort at this little-used country house for years, forgotten by his Lord. The face of shock he pulled on opening the door to a well-dressed young gentleman, entirely unannounced and without any retinue, made Sterling alarmed for the fellow's health.

"Yes, my Lord?" he asked, more in confusion than curiosity. "How may I be of er, assistance?"

"Is Lady Duckington in residence?" Sterling asked, without a second's pause.

"Er, yes, yes, I believe she is." the man replied, still completely bemused.

"Excellent, thank you. Please be kind enough to arrange someone to walk my horse – he's had a long and wearing ride." Toulon, well trained and tired, stood where he was, as Sterling dropped his reins over a convenient decoration beside the base of the stairs.

Moving swiftly past the footman, taking enough care not to barge the geriatric servant aside, but not tarrying with any further formalities, he asked "Where might I find my Lady?" he asked as he went.

"But my lord!" The footman made a faltering objection, but Sterling halted the protest with a glance, and waited. "Er…. In the Drawing Room, my Lord…." The footman waved vaguely towards the rear of the house and did not offer any further resistance.

Sterling tore rapidly through the front rooms, with no idea where he was going, but a very sure notion of what (in fact who) he was searching for. He found himself passing through the billiards room, which looked like it had seen little use of late, most likely due to the infirmity of the late Viscount. Abandoning that smoky little den, he quickly moved on to the library, which was occupied only by a chambermaid, and several hundred volumes of undisturbed books, mostly encyclopaedias and editions of Hansard's.

Letting out a small groan of frustration, he propelled himself rapidly down a short corridor, flung open a set of doors with a melodrama that would have been excessive even for the west end stage, and found himself in a well-lit drawing room, standing before Lady Amelia Duckington, at least as beautiful in the flesh as she had been in his memory, wearing a widow's black gown and leafing gently through a novel.

"Lady Duckington" he spoke decisively.

"Sterling" she replied, seeming somehow detached and far less surprised than he had anticipated. "What a pleasant surprise. What brings you down to Springden this fair afternoon?"

"Urgent business. I am to convey you immediately to London."

"Has war broken out again?" she said, cattily, mocking him despite her better instincts. Men could be so pompous when they were caught up in some cause or another.

"Do not tarry. I come on..." and words suddenly failed him. He saw Amelia rising to her feet, stepping towards him, and realised what he already knew, that this was the most wonderful woman that he ever known, and he was here not so much on a legalistic errand, but simply to see her, to be with her, to hold her and kiss her and make something tangible once more of their fragmentary affair.

"On what, my lord?" she said, running her hand down his face, over the fine stubble beginning to darken his skin. The touch was sensual and sent a shock of desire through both of them. The human contact brought Sterling rapidly to his senses.

"- on urgent business. You must return to London at once, your house is being usurped."

"Usurped?" she said, again without the desperate surprise he had expected to hear in her voice. To him, it seemed that she had drifted off into a sort of dream world here, mourning in perpetuity, alone with her thoughts. It made him only more determined to snap her out of it and drag her back into the world, through sheer force of masculine will if necessary.

She turned from him a moment, sighing. *'So,'* she thought, *'it has come to this already. Redmayne tires of trying to woo me, and has turned to worse tactics.'*

"Pray tell, what do you mean" Amelia's voice shook a little as she asked.

"What the devil do you think? That rotter Redmayne. If I'd had my way, he'd be driven through the streets of London to be flogged like a petty thief, but instead I'm here to take you back to London, so that we can stop him in a more…. polite…. way." She turned away from him again. She still seemed so serene, almost ghostly in her heavy black dress. She looked out towards the duck pond, still, betraying almost nothing, seemingly undisturbed by man or beast, whilst inside, she was all turmoil.

"I shan't go. I shan't go and I don't care for the consequences." She turned back to him now, away from the duck pond, peering at him with her sad, blue-violet eyes. "I appreciate you coming here Sterling. It is good to know that you care for my welfare, very good indeed. But my place is here now. I am a widow, and it is a widow's place to mourn. The consequences to my property do not concern me. I…. I have made my decision – nothing he can do will make me marry him, and if that means losing everything that I have, so be it."

Even as she said this, her voice faltered, which indicated to Sterling that she did not entirely mean what she had said, that she could still be brought back into this world with some action, with the love of a good man. And he was that man, for he knew, in that instant, that he loved her.

Sterling stepped forward, and took her by the hand.

"Enough of this nonsense…" he said, with a frustrated sigh, and pulled her into his arms. He kissed her assertively, with a soft touch but a depth of intensity that communicated all that still needed to be said, all that he still felt unable to put into words.

Amelia melted against him, returning the kiss with passion, feeling her body warm throughout, and an aching physical need take hold of her. It confused her, even as it thrilled her. She was supposed to be grieving, to not think of such things, yet, more than anything else at this moment, she wanted this man.

It came to her that he was the strongest, most open and honest man that she had ever met, and the only one who had ever had the courage to truly stand his ground in her presence. He had never been easy to manipulate, like all of the shallow fools who had desired her body, yet his dominance came with obvious care – demonstrated yet again by the fact that he was here, now, for her. It was thrilling to be held by him, to be kissed by him, to feel his strong touch on her body, creating a warmth that penetrated the sad, heavy layers of her black mourning gown, and the fog of dark emotional exhaustion that matched it. She had needed this, and he completed it all by saying.

"I know that you'll come with me, Amelia. Somehow, I've always known. I need you – I want you with me, as I have never wanted another woman. These last many weeks have made that abundantly clear to me. Come, we must pack your things." He led her from the room, and she followed.

There was, in that moment, no more that needed words.

They reached her chamber, but rather than beginning to gather her possessions, she turned to him, reached for him, and pulling him to her, kissed him with a depth of passion that rocked him to the core. He knew that time was short, that he should pull away, and make certain that they left for London as soon as possible, yet he found that impossible to do.

"Amelia" he groaned her name against her lips, as her hands ran over his body, proving to her that he was there, that he was real, and not a figment of her troubled dreams. Amelia realised that she wanted him now, that she needed the physical reassurance of his body, after so long trapped in a nightmare. His control failed him, and he pulled her to him, his hands seeking the lacing of her dress, his kisses covering her face, her neck, the delectable curve of her shoulder, revealed as the dress fell away.

Her heart pounding, and her breath coming short, she reached for his clothes, desperate to feel his skin beneath her hands, his body against hers, to cast herself utterly into his control, and let his passion sweep her away, even if only for a little while. Months of repressed desire rose up in both of them and they abandoned themselves to one another, seeking the oldest solace known to man. The world and all its petty worries, avaricious cousins, prudent lawyers, the prying eyes of servants and the best-laid plans of mothers all drifted off into the ether.

Soon, Sterling found himself buried entirely in Amelia's person, plunging himself into her womanhood with wild abandon, holding her down hard as he did, delighting in her cries of passionate encouragement. His natural instinct for aggressive passion took over completely.

She was responsive, like a coiled spring, her passion a demanding force, driven higher by his sure control of their loving, as if the fact that he restrained her was what allowed her to let herself go completely, and revel in the sensations. He held her, pinning her down, undeterred by the remaining layers of clothing, which they had pushed aside in their haste, and she relented entirely, slipping into the blissful surrender to another's control.

His hands on her body drove her, spurring her on to greater intensity, and pleasure. She had never experienced anything quite like this before, a forcefulness strong enough to create sensations close to pain, that transformed on the instant into a pleasure beyond any she had known, but she knew at once that she liked it. It gave her renewed lust, as all that had been repressed in her vigil here at Springden, all the sadness and grief and sense of loss was forgotten, was released in a glorious burst of pleasure.

It was a gift that he gave her with his strength. Yes, that was it! Had she stopped to think about it, she would have drawn that conclusion. It was not just for himself that he was firm and strong in their bedplay, but for her as well, and he gave her strength in doing it. Nothing before had drawn such a powerful response from her. She reached her peak as he drove her further than she had ever gone before, and she was left lying beneath him, trembling, quivering and gasping for breath.

There was no guilt this time. The shame of adultery in the past had given her a low thrill, a basic sense of pleasure, but now, with her husband having passed away, after blessing her future happiness and giving her license to be happy and free, she felt finally able to abandon herself, give herself fully to a man.

She had not, really, realised before that she had been carrying that guilt – it was only in its lack that she understood it.

This felt incredible. She writhed and gasped her way through numerous little deaths, her skin tingling, her nipples hard at attention, her womanhood throbbing violently, until finally Sterling was spent, and they could lie, panting and overcome with a shared satisfaction, on the bed, in each other's arms.

"I think I shall relent, as you have suggested I would," Lady Duckington said at last, a gentle laugh in her voice "It is high time I surrendered to your authority, my good Marquess Hemsbridge."

"Of a certainty, my Lady" said Sterling, chuckling and rolling back over her, languidly, laying leisurely kisses on her exposed skin. "Someone has to lay down the law, and it might as well be me" and on the final syllable, he slapped her thigh gently, reddening it slightly, as she gasped, arched against him, and pulled him down into another kiss.

"Oh, I should say so" Lady Duckington said. "- and after all, it isn't every day one inherits a fully furnished townhouse in London. It would be a terrible shame to have it simply slip from my grasp" she caressed his face, tracing her fingers over his bluff features, his hard jaw, his sharply defined cheekbones, his slight hint of stubble after the hard ride that had brought him here.

"Then let us collect your necessary belongings and be gone to London." Sterling made to rise to his feet. Amelia extended her hand, and gently pulled him back down towards her.

"Not so fast" she smiled. "I'm not sure we're quite finished here yet..."

An hour later, restored to respectability, and with a minimum of Amelia's bags packed, they descended the staircase to arrange for her other possessions to be sent on after them, and to partake of a quick light meal, whilst Amelia's carriage was prepared. Toulon would remain here, until Sterling could arrange to collect him, or send his groom to do so.

They arrived at the house in Burton Lane in a decisive mood, prepared for whatever difficulty they might face, having collected Mr Runciman on their way. Jenkins answered the door, for which Sterling was grateful. It gave him the opportunity to quickly discuss matters with the faithful old butler, who had served his Lady so well.

"My Lord!" he had exclaimed on opening the door, perhaps hoping that it would be him, and so taking on this task usually reserved for more junior staff members. "You have returned! And with my Lady in attendance as well! And Mr Runciman! Oh heavens, this is marvellous news!"

"Comport yourself, Jenkins" Sterling spoke in the tone an army officer might reserve for a faltering troop of cavalry. "Is Redmayne, Viscount Duckington, in the house?"

"Oh sir, he has hardly been away! Why in all of your absence my Lady, he has hardly given us a moment's peace! He has already had the footmen re-orient the billiards room according to his own designs, and I fear he has similar plans for the dining room and guest rooms as well! Why, he is positively taking over already, as if you mean nothing!"

"And with my husband's coffin barely settled in the earth. My god, it's just too terrible for words."

"There is nothing else for it. We must confront him forthwith. Lead on Jenkins!" and at Sterling's firm words of command, the four of them stepped boldly into the house, Mr Runciman looking rather nervous, but determined.

*

Alfred Redmayne was standing in the Drawing Room by himself, admiring his new acquisition. It was as he had always wanted in a London townhouse - high ceiling and tall windows, with floors and tables polished to a sheen, the very model of cosmopolitan elegance.

'All I need to go with all this' he thought to himself slyly, *'- is a nice, pretty young wife to sit by the window sewing all day, to obey me in all matters.'* He chuckled at the thought of the ravishing Lady Duckington. She would be his, and soon. He had decided it, and he was a man used to getting what he wanted.

Once she had returned from her self-imposed exile in the country, she would be his, for surely, no woman would choose poverty over marriage to a wealthy man.

Certainly not one as loose with her favours as lady Duckington had been.

He had even taken the trouble of purchasing a ring in advance of her return. It was an excellent ring, bought in Holborn from an old Jewish merchant who specialised in these sorts of things. He had reassured Redmayne, who knew almost nothing of the minds of women, that it was exactly the sort that would please his bride to be.

There was a sizeable, finely cut diamond set into the top if it, a ship sailing tall and proud on a sea of pale gold. It was ideal, nestled in a little box on a bed of velvet, and he could not wait to woo her with it. She would give in, he was confident of that. Women were simple creatures, his father had always told him. Show them something shiny and they're yours. He yearned to test this theory, and then to have Amelia and her body all to himself.

The door flew open unexpectedly, and Redmayne fumbled to return the ring to his pocket. In stepped Jenkins, the butler, with his hang-dog expression and the sort of discreet manner which most aristocrats favour but which Redmayne found he could not trust. He had expected the ageing servant to make some announcement or other, but instead, he merely held the door open for three other figures to come striding confidently in. Jenkins announced them, as he was charged to, but he needn't have bothered.

"My Lord, may I present, The Marquess of Hemsbridge, the Lady of the House, Lady Duckington, and the solicitor, Mr Runciman."

"Yes, yes I know who they are!" Redmayne exclaimed impatiently. "That will be all, Jenkins!" He did rather wonder what Runciman was doing here, though.

"As my lord desires" said the butler, neatly closing the doors behind him as he left. Redmayne swivelled on his feet and smiled. Amelia had returned, and she was no longer in full mourning! She had changed into a pleasant gown of a navy colour, which would suitably classify as half mourning, but flattered her delightful figure very nicely. But what the devil was Hemsbridge doing here? The presence of this large, handsome, and well-endowed man of estates made him anxious, as did the presence of Mr Runciman, for whom he could see no earthly need at this juncture, but he tried to hide it behind a smile and played the host.

"So, my Lady Duckington" he said, in his reedy voice with a slight Scottish inflection. "You have seen fit to return to the capital. I trust your stay in Berkshire was to your satisfaction?"

"It was my lord, thank you. It is pleasant indeed to return to one's own residence after a sojourn in the country."

"Indeed it is!" Redmayne said. "Although I should think that, if you wish to continue to enjoy such a pleasure, you'd best acquire another residence, or else submit to certain, conditions that the master of this house chooses to impose."

"What the devil are you speaking of Redmayne!?" said Hemsbridge, clenching his fists and stepping forward somewhat menacingly. At this, Redmayne could not help but recoil instinctively in fear, a most unbecoming act for an English Viscount.

"Now now, my good Lord Hemsbridge, there's no need to be churlish, especially not towards your host! And besides, you shall address me by my proper title if you please!"

"You are not my host, Duckington." Sterling said the final word with contempt, to a man who had already brought nothing but dishonour to his newly inherited house. "I beseech you to study the correct legal documentation, wherein, you shall find that in fact, we two are both guests of Lady Duckington here!"

"Oh I would not be so sure, my lord!" Redmayne replied, licking his lips in a most unappealing gesture. "For you see, if you were to study said papers more fully, as I have, you would discover that in fact, Lady Duckington's possession of the house is conditional on her spending adequate time here, and, following that, on her finding a husband of suitable rank and title... which is where I step in."

"Surely... no, surely you do not expect...!" but, even as he said these words, Hemsbridge was forced to watch aghast as Alfred Redmayne, Viscount Duckington, produced from his pocket a splendid diamond ring.

"Lady Duckington, would you do me the honour of accepting my hand in marriage, and thereby retaining your full estates?"

Amelia gasped. It was a real gasp, forced out of her in a moment she had not anticipated and could not react to with anything but unguarded honesty. She knew – he had, after all, asked her repeatedly, that Redmayne wanted to marry her, but to have him ask her formally, and in such words! Both men heard it, and as the breath was being forced from her, snapped their heads to look at her, and ponder her reaction.

"Good grief! This is... not what I expected... I have told you before, sir, that I do not wish to marry you!" she shook, angry, reeling at his gall and greed. Redmayne stepped forward, and tried to pull her to him.

"I know that you may not be overcome with passion for me at this early stage. We are after all, little acquainted. But I feel that, given time, a certain… closeness… may develop between us. And surely you wish the security of knowing that you will be supported by a wealthy man, the certainty that you will be able to continue living in the homes that you are used to? I cannot imagine that you are foolish enough to choose abject poverty."

She pushed him away, faltered, dizzy, suddenly unsure of everything. What should she do? What was there to do? She had to have the house, and she was used, after all, to the companionship of marriage – but… she loathed this man – if only it were Sterling before her, asking her to marry him!

Sterling watched, barely believing his eyes.

"Come, my Lady, my Amelia. You know in your heart that it makes sense. It is the only possible way for you to keep your lifestyle and wealth. Who else would marry you, with the reputation that you have so cleverly created for yourself? None of the high and mighty Lords will, that is for certain!"

"Oh I wouldn't be so sure of that," said Sterling, his tone an odd mix of amusement and anger, as he stepped forward, before bowing over Amelia's hand.

Amelia gasped again, struggling to believe what she was seeing, for surely, she must be dreaming, if Sterling truly meant what he had just implied!

What a remarkable turn of events! What was happening? Was the Marquess of Hemsbridge truly about to propose?

"Amelia, my dear, I know that our ship has not always sailed the easiest course. I know that I can be something of a hot-head, a braggart, a little over-bearing and far too intense. Yet I know in my heart that there is no other woman for me, and, if you feel for me even a fraction of the passion that I feel for you, then marry me, and settle all of this once and for all."

Redmayne spluttered, red in the face, and obviously angry.

He thought to speak, but was quelled by a stern look from Mr Runciman, who was rather enjoying this conclusion to the matter.

Amelia faltered a moment, unsure if she had truly heard those words, then rushed forward clasping Sterling's hands, with the most joyous smile she had ever displayed in her life.

"Oh Sterling! My Sterling! Of course I will marry you!"

And Alfred Redmayne, having the good sense to know that he was now, most definitely beaten, with this all witnessed by Runciman, rose to his feet, glared at them with a false smile at the joy shared between the couple before him, and left the house forever, with his head held high.

"Jenkins, you may send my things on to me" was the entirety of Redmayne's farewell to them all.

Behind him, as he exited the room, Sterling and Amelia stepped into a passionate embrace, and began a kiss that would go on for some time yet.

*

Jenkins, after ensuring that the front door was solidly closed on the back of Redmayne, turned, and discreetly shut the drawing room door as well, leaving the lovers to their embrace, and proceeded belowstairs to tell the staff the good news.

The wedding came, several months later, as the grand unveiling of this new couple, Amelia liberated at last from her mourning clothes, Sterling finally ending his time as a bachelor, to the delight of many, but the disappointment of some. There were several young ladies and gentlemen, on both sides of the aisle who were privately disappointed to see two such attractive and eligible people taken forever off the marriage market, but they did not show their displeasure, and the day was a happy one for all who attended. Quite a number of Amelia's past lovers were amongst the guests, and she was pleased to see that it seemed they all looked upon her fondly – a better outcome than might have been expected, in the circumstances.

The wedding took place in a modest church, close to Springden Chase.

It was decided that that was the best place for it, as it was both easily accessible to all guests, and had a certain sentimental value, being the place where they had first felt truly able to be a couple, to express their feelings for one another, and to admit, to any degree, their love.

Today, at the humble parish church of St. Mary-le-Bow in Springden village, that love reached the point of fruition.

Casting glances about the church at the assembled throng, Sterling could not help but be moved by the huge array of friends and acquaintances who had made the journey to Berkshire for the wedding.

There was Stanningfield, his shock of black hair standing out against the pale dresses of the women all around him, casting dark glances at the prettiest of them despite being a happily married man. Next to him was his bride, Catherine, beaming joy at all the world and holding their baby girl, Henrietta, close.

On the other side of the aisle was Captain Westbury, resplendent in his full uniform of the guards, and firmly holding the hand of his beloved Blanchette, the hand he had famously fought a duel to win.

Just in front of them was an old drinking companion of Sterling's, Richard Maitland, Viscount Bellham, still looking happy as the day he had first fallen for a serving girl, Anna Perkins, and married her for love.

She seemed to have taken to her new situation remarkably well, and despite her humble origins was displaying all the hallmarks of her ancestry, chattering away with lifelong nobles like it was the most natural thing in the world.

Surveying the crowd as he awaited Amelia's arrival, Sterling's eye suddenly fell upon the blonde hair and pretty visage of Lady Charlotte, whom he had briefly attempted to pursue some time ago, a period which had included a rather inappropriate incident in a garden. He had rather dreaded this moment, and in fact had rather hoped that Lady Charlotte might not come to the wedding at all, despite her invitation, but here she was, in full view, near the front and pressed close to Don Diego, the Argentine Count who had won her affections, despite Sterling's effort to do the same.

But to Sterling's surprise, and immense delight, the couple were not hostile towards him, nor did they recoil in embarrassment on realising he was looking at them, but rather they smiled, and nodded, and indicated quietly the depth of their satisfaction at being here. This filled him with a great warmth, and he nodded kindly at Don Diego to indicate that there were no hard feelings between the two of them.

Sterling almost gasped in amazement as he realised that James Blackwood was here! He had briefly fraternized with the notorious rogue in his youth, but had long since lost contact, partly as a result of his mother's insistence on preserving the family's humour. He had, of course, heard that the notorious cad was now allegedly a reformed character, that he had fallen back in love with an old flame, married, and changed his ways, but he had not entirely believed the stories until now.

Blackwood looked healthier than he had ever seen him look, colour and substance had returned to his once sallow cheeks, his hair was thick and his eyes shining. The woman, Honour, was beautiful and dignified, with a shock of red-gold hair and pleasing, sculpted features.

Despite himself he was happy to see that Blackwood, of all people, also seemed to have found happiness.

And then, finally, of course, there was his mother, seated, a little unexpectedly, next to Professor Edward Greenidge. She had, of course, pretended to object to this match, she had felt almost duty-bound to, given Amelia's reputation, but it was clear that in her heart, she knew that it was right, and now she could do nothing but beam joy back at Sterling.

He noted her hand wandering towards the arm of the eccentric old professor, and the strange thought came to him that there might be a growing affection between the two. But these thoughts were interrupted by his best man, Aldercott, whom he had long forgiven for his assignations with Amelia, coming over and slapping his back in a jocular fashion.

"Well, congratulations are in order old chap!" Aldercott said good-naturedly.

"Thanks old boy" replied Sterling. "No hard feelings eh? Considering the two of you once.....?"

"Oh, absolutely none, my good fellow, none whatsoever. I'll admit, I was a little fond of Lady Duckington at one point, but not nearly enough to bally well marry her!"

"Well that settles that then!" whispered Sterling in satisfaction. "Do you have the ring?"

"Of course! Right here in my breast pocket."

"Wonderful." At that moment the organist began, the church doors swung open, and the most beautiful woman Sterling had ever known walked into the room, looking more radiant than ever in her stunning wedding dress.

'*Yes*' thought Sterling, overcome with happiness '*I think things are set to be alright from here on in. Marriage doesn't look so bad after all.*'

About the Author

Arietta Richmond has been a compulsive reader and writer all her life. Whilst her reading has covered an enormous range of topics, history has always fascinated her, and historical novels been amongst her favourite reading.

She has written a wide range of work, from business articles and other non-fiction works (published under a pen name) but fiction has always been a major part of her life. Now, her Regency Historical Romance books are finally being released. The Derbyshire Set is comprised of 10 shorter novels (6 released so far). The 'His Majesty's Hounds' series is comprised of 10 novels, with the fifth having just been released.

She also has a standalone longer novel shortly to be released, and two other series of novels in development.

She lives in Australia, and when not reading or writing, likes to travel, and to see in person the places where history happened.

Be the first to know about it when Arietta's next book is released!

Sign up to Arietta's newsletter at

http://www.ariettarichmond.com

When you do, you will receive a free copy of the <u>subscriber exclusive</u> novella **'A Gift of Love',** a prequel to the Derbyshire Set series, which ends on the day that 'The Earl's Unexpected Bride' begins

This story is not for sale anywhere – it is absolutely exclusive to newsletter subscribers!

Other Books in 'The Derbyshire Set'

Available at all good book stores and for ebook readers too!

Coming Soon!

Here is your preview of the next book in 'The Derbyshire Set' by Arietta Richmond

The Derbyshire Set ~ Book 7

Regency Historical Romance

Arietta Richmond

Olivia Asterwood, Marchioness Hemsbridge, smiled politely at her host, all the while wishing that she were anywhere else but here, in yet another ballroom. Balls had ceased to be entertaining, even with the opportunity that they provided for gossip, and discovering yet more secrets of the family histories of the *ton*. She was heartily sick of watching her stubborn son dismiss every potential candidate for wife.

She sighed, quietly, and tried to concentrate on the conversation. She had already made one unforgivable faux-pas, just a few moments ago, and felt deeply embarrassed by her lapse. So shaken was she, that she actually needed the cane that she carried, for once.

Her host, however, was a very forgiving man, she had to admit. He was cheerfully discussing the style and furnishings of this, his new townhouse, as if her faux-pas had never happened.

Her son was standing beside her, looking amused at her discomfiture - she suspected that he had barely prevented himself from laughing. She would have something to say about that, later!

Her host, Viscount Bellham, was speaking again.

"The décor is, I'm afraid, a little drab for my tastes. I prefer the subtle elegance that has recently come into fashion in the West End, though I suppose this ballroom is pleasant enough."

"Indeed it is sir!" declared Lady Hemsbridge, her eyes wide as she tried to display appropriate polite interest in the conversation.

She gestured sweepingly, taking in the whole room, from the high windows on the back wall to the austere family portraits which lined the side, via the vast crystal chandelier that hung over their heads.

"And, in fact, I rather think that it becomes you better to remain rooted in longer established fashions. Why, if all of us exclusively followed the latest fads and newest styles, then none of us would have any energy, money, or indeed, good sense left over! Sometimes the old ways are the best, even if you young gentlemen don't believe it to be so."

"I er, er, er, find that I quite agree with your sentiments, my er, lady" interjected a newcomer, whom Lady Hemsbridge had ever encountered before. His willingness to so blatantly break with social convention, and join a conversation with someone to whom he had not been introduced, rather shocked her, yet she found herself interested in his words, nonetheless.

"You are quite right. Without the, er, er inheritance of previous generations' expertise and good labours, we would all er, be quite lost! Traditions, like great houses, must er, er, persist, what?"

Lady Hemsbridge eyed the new arrival curiously. He was a slim man, and rather tall, with a hooked nose and slightly beady eyes that looked like they'd spent a little too much time peering into obscure books.

He wore a brass pince-nez and unfashionable clothes, but he had a full head of dark hair, and the air of a man who had once been quite spectacularly handsome, without even realising it.

For that matter, he was still rather handsome – she thought, rather wryly, that he appeared to have matured like a good wine, and achieved a greater polish with age.

Lady Hemsbridge could not help but be quite taken with him.

"My apologies my Lady, I do not believe that the two of you have been introduced..." Bellham cut in rather smoothly, smoothing the cuffs of his dark green superfine dress coat in a single movement.

"Lady Hemsbridge, may I present to you Professor Edward Greenidge, of the Royal College of Arms, a most learned fellow, and, as the researcher who demonstrated my wife's noble inheritance, the man to whom I am more grateful than anyone else on earth."

"My Lord is most er, gracious in his praises. My achievement was quite incidental, you must understand, though I er, er accept the compliment graciously."

"Professor, I present Lady Hemsbridge, and her son, the Marquess Hemsbridge."

"Why…" said Lady Hemsbridge, growing more fascinated by the man "…. Greenidge? Sir, are you perchance, the son of Viscount and Lady Camberton, late of the county of Somerset?"

"The very same" he said, with a resigned, scholarly air. "Alas, I am all that remains of my immediate family, save my brother Reginald, the current Viscount, who is not of good health. I devote myself now whole-heartedly to er, er my studies. But tell me, er, my lady, how have you come by er, er, such a great knowledge of er, er, the great houses of England as to identify me so swiftly? Few these days have heard of er, my family, as we have not prospered so much in recent generations, and our estates are small…"

"Well, I may not be a scholar of the College of Arms, my good Mr. Greenidge, but I am something of an enthusiastic amateur in questions of family history, if you would not think it impudent of me to make such a boast." Olivia was aware that this was not quite how her friends in Society would describe her interest in family histories.

She flushed at the thought that the ladies of the *ton* would more likely have said that she was an inveterate gossip, who liked nothing better than discovering skeletons in the closets of family bloodlines.

The flush stained her cheeks a delicate rose, and the sparkle in her eyes from her genuine interest in the subject made it quite visible how stunningly beautiful she had been in her youth – and how much of that beauty remained, now.

She was completely unaware of this effect – but it was not lost on Professor Greenidge.

✱✱✱

"Indeed not, My Lady!" Professor Greenidge almost bounced on the spot at this news. At last, he thought, someone who shared his passion! And a lady to boot, of, he suspected, a similar age to himself, but still distinctly charming with her youthful beauty not, by any means, completely faded!

Before he could say anything further, she was enthusiastically asking questions of him, seeking to plumb his great depths of knowledge.

"Now tell me Mr. Greenidge, for I've always been concerned to know more, the House of d'Allemberd…."

In her enthusiasm, and without any thought as to who might be watching, she took him by the arm and led him away from her son and host, towards some chairs nestled beside the potted palms, in the corner of the ballroom, leaving the two younger men to exchange a knowing grin, and a shrug of surprise.

Edward acquiesced to this surprising action with good grace, as caught up in their conversation as she was, and, never having particularly cared what society thought of him, utterly oblivious to the fact that this might be noted as in any way unusual.

He was usually somewhat uncomfortable at society occasions, finding that he had nothing in common with any of those who attended, and absolutely no ability at small talk.

His hesitance of speech, which was unimportant to other scholars, was looked down upon by the *ton*, who did not tolerate imperfection well. Yet, with this Lady, all of that fell away – he ceased to be aware of the passing of time, completely engaged with the conversation.

Their conversation travelled deep into the entangled paths of inheritance, and centuries of the history of the upper ten thousand. He was entranced by her knowledge, and shocked to discover how much she had come to know through the capturing of snippets of gossip, and subsequent diligent research that proved that gossip true, or not. It put a whole new light on what there was to be known, and on what the rather formal tomes that he studied might have left out. He found himself with a hunger to know more, the same hunger that he felt, on discovering an ancient book, previously though lost.

And, as obsessive as he was, he had to admit that, as a man, he was not immune to her charms, as a woman. He flinched away from those thoughts – only once in his life had he truly allowed a woman into his life, and the pain of remembering was too much to bear. So he pushed all consideration aside, of anything other than her delightful knowledge of the lineages of the nobility. Conversation on his favourite topic went a long way to assuaging some of the sense of loneliness, which he had not truly realised he felt, until now.

✳✳✳

The clearing of a throat beside her, followed by a delicate tap on her shoulder, brought Olivia back to awareness of her location.

She gasped as she realised that she sat in Viscount Bellham's ballroom, with the *ton* swirling about the room in front of her. Her son, Sterling Asterwood, the current Marquess Hemsbridge, was waiting for her attention to focus on him.

"Mother, it is rather late, and I find myself fatigued by this evening's entertainment. I fear I must conclude that you have found far better conversation than I have." He smiled at her expression, knowing full well that, for once in his life, he had her speechless.

"It is my intention to call for the carriage, and retire for the evening – will you be returning with me?"

Dazed, Olivia was stunned to realise that she had spent some hours deep in conversation with Professor Greenidge, so engaged by his knowledge and his willingness to discuss her obsession, that she had not noticed the time pass. Even more startling, she had not observed Sterling's interactions with the fluttering crowd of hopeful young women, all of whom wished to capture him in marriage.

She chided herself for her lapse in attention – finding a bride for Sterling was her primary aim in life at this point. It was critical that the Hemsbridge line continue, that he marry, and produce an heir. How could she have failed in her duty so egregiously? Shaking herself out of her daze, she regarded Sterling a moment, before regally inclining her head in agreement.

"Certainly, it does seem an appropriate point at which to depart – I will be with you momentarily."

Lady Hemsbridge turned to Professor Greenidge, smiling.

"I must thank you, sir, for an evening of most compelling conversation. I have not enjoyed a discussion so much in a very long time. And I must commend your amazing depth of knowledge – never before have a met such a learned scholar on the families of the nobility."

"My Lady is, er, too kind. I must return the compliment, for your knowledge is, er, er, also impressively extensive. I hope that we may converse again, at some point in the future."

Lady Hemsbridge rose, as did the Professor, who bent, with surprising elegance, to kiss her hand in farewell. Olivia turned, and proceeded towards their host, to bid him good evening. Her son, the Marquess, gave the Professor a smile and a bow, scooped up the cane that she had quite forgotten, and followed her.

***

Settled in the carriage on the way home, Olivia pondered the evening. She had definitely not been herself, it had been almost, an unmitigated disaster, from the faux-pas in front of their host, to forgetting her primary need to find Sterling a wife, to that last little disaster of forgetting her cane, which had, of course, provided an opportunity for the gossips of the *ton* to realise that it was an affectation, nothing more.

The only redeeming thing had been that remarkable conversation with Professor Greenidge. He had seemed gauche at the start, but she had rapidly warmed to him. Idly, she wondered if she would ever see him again. Another conversation like that would be wonderful!

Jamison opened the door promptly, as Edward reached the top of the steps. Nodding his thanks, Edward handed him his coat and hat, and stepped into the marble floored foyer. The echo of his steps came back to him, emphasising the size, and emptiness, of the house.

Reginald kept the house up, but had not been here for quite some time, as his illnesses plagued him, and his interest in London society diminished. It was convenient for Edward, giving him somewhere of his own to stay, in London, whilst attending various functions at Viscount Bellham's invitation, and the staff were happy to have someone to look after. He feared he was a sad disappointment to them, however.

He came, in their eyes, shockingly unattended, with only his valet of many years to assist him – and that a luxury which he was all too aware that most Professors would not be able to afford.

Usually, he was glad of the peace and quiet, of a chance to have the place to himself, with no need to attend upon anyone else's conversation or expectations – but, tonight, the house felt odd – almost as if he could sense the fact that no-one else was here, except the discreet and nearly invisible servants, who were, no doubt, ensconced in the warm kitchen, belowstairs.

Edward settled in his favourite chair in the library, with a warming glass of brandy, and settled back to let the tensions of dealing with social interaction fade away. Surprised, he realised that he was much more relaxed than he normally felt after dealing with other people. His eyes drifted along the shelves. The books called to him – there was so much he had yet to learn, about so many families of the *ton*!

He wanted to lift the books down, to drag out specific references, and to dig into his research, following the tantalising clues that the Marchioness' conversation had provided him. Her face came to his mind, smiling, animated as she spoke of lineages and history with as much passion as he felt for it himself. That passionate enthusiasm made her shine – she was quite beautiful when she spoke so, with a quality and strength that far outshone the insipid 'beauties' that the gentlemen all seemed to admire.

He was shocked at his own thoughts – never did he look at women that way, not since Sarina. He pushed that thought away, as the old pain tried to surface, and brought his mind firmly back to the intriguing histories of the highest families in the land. He would save the research for tomorrow, would allow himself an indulgent day in this library, with the books that filled it.

Almost everything here, Reginald, never much of a reader, had bought for Edward's benefit. A gentleman was supposed to have a good library, and Reginald had been happy to allow his brother to stock it with whatever held his interest. To do this new line of research justice, he would need many hours, and a clear head.

Tossing back the last of the brandy, he took himself off to bed.

****

Keller assisted him to ready for bed, then hurried away, clutching the evening's clothes. Edward knew that Keller's obsessive nature would ensure that they were cleaned, and in perfect readiness for when they were next needed.

He settled himself in the warmed bed, and closed his eyes. Sleep did not come. Instead, the silence of the house, broken only by the shifting of the log in the fireplace, pressed in on him. He felt strange, he reached for a word to describe the feeling, and the one that seemed to fit, was 'lonely'. His eyes shot open at the thought. He, who had been so self-contained, so comfortable in his bachelorhood, his research his only need, for so many years – why would he think of loneliness now?

Yet lonely he was. The emptiness of the house seemed an echo of the emptiness of so much of his life. He pushed the thoughts away, chiding himself for imaginative silliness. He was just tired, he generally hated social events, as he always felt so out of place, so inept in dealing with the sharp edges behind the smiling faces of the *ton*. That was it, this was all a result of tiredness, and the morning would bring more sensible thoughts again.

On that thought, he turned on his side, closed his eyes, and determined that he would sleep. His mind, however, did not co-operate. The image that rose behind his eyelids was, again, the Marchioness' face, as she spoke with him this evening. Never had he spent so long talking to one person before, and certainly never a woman, highly placed in society.

As he drifted, finally, towards sleep, the last thought he was aware of was, again, a recognition of how attractive she was, of the remarkable energy that she had brought to every word.

****

Edward woke refreshed, and looking forward to his day. He forced himself to partake of a hearty breakfast, before proceeding to the library, and the delights of his research – for he was very well aware that, once he began, it was most likely that he would forget to eat, forget anything else, until the darkness outside the windows made him aware that night had fallen.

He closed the library door, laid out his papers and pens, drew his journal from its drawer in the desk, and simply stood, appreciating what was before him, for a moment. The room was beautiful – large, with shelves lining the walls, from floor to the high ceiling, a tall ladder providing access to the upper sections. The windows were tall and elegant, allowing warm light to fall across the desk. Leather bound volumes filled the shelves, and a few stood stacked on a side table, where he had left them for easy reference.

Rooms like this, more than any one place, were his home.

He reached for the books, and began.

Hours later, having filled pages of his journal with notes, and with many books spread out across the furniture, open at specific pages, or with multiple pages marked, Edward paused. For the umpteenth time, he thought *'I must ask the Marchioness about that – she appeared to know more than I do, and more than I can find in these books, about that family.'*

He made another note on a separate list, adding to the tally of questions. He looked at it, and shook his head. He might never see the woman again – and here he was making a list of questions to ask her! Yet he kept making the list. For the thought that he would never see her again was uncomfortable, not something he wished to contemplate. Surely he could find a way. Bellham would help him.

It was all for the good of his research, just that, he had no interest in seeing her again for any other reason, he assured himself, even as the image of her vivacious face, surrounded by rich dark auburn hair, only lightly touched with grey, filled his mind. He went back to the books, trying, but failing, to forget how she looked.

He worked through the day, unaware of anything outside the room, and his thoughts – thoughts that, rebelliously, kept coming back to the Marchioness, as well as to the very interesting questions that she had raised about the lineages that he was studying.

By the time that night fell, and Jamison came to inform him that dinner was served, Edward had created a huge chart of the lineage of two key families. For this, he used a long, wide scroll – these were made expressly for him, his one true extravagance.

Making one last annotation on its length, he placed it carefully to allow the ink to dry, and followed Jamison from the room. It was imperative that he meet the Marchioness again – he needed her knowledge to resolve some key questions. And he had so much to show her – he knew that she would be enraptured by what he had discovered – he could imagine her face, when he showed her!

Get

"The Marchioness' Second Chance"

as soon as it's released – go to

http://www.ariettarichmond.com

and make sure that you are signed up for news and release notices !

Books in the 'His Majesty's Hounds' Series

Redeeming the Marquess (coming soon)

Healing Lord Barton (coming soon)

Winning the Merchant Earl (coming soon)

Loving the Bitter Baron (coming soon)

Rescuing the Countess (coming soon)

Attracting the Spymaster (coming soon)

Other Books from Dreamstone Publishing

Dreamstone publishes books in a wide variety of categories – here are some of our other bestselling books:-

We have books in many categories, ranging from Erotica and Romance to Kids Books, Books on Writing, Business Books, Photography, Cook Books, Diaries, Coloring books and much more. New books are released each month.

Be the first to know when our next books are coming out

Be first to get all the news – sign up for our newsletter at

http://www.dreamstonepublishing.com